DEAD MAN DRAW

Retired lawman Dan Shaw and veteran gunfighter Tom ride into the sprawling town of Dead Man Draw. Quickly hired as sheriff and deputy, and charged with collecting protection money from town businesses, it doesn't take long to discover why their appointments were so hasty — the place is crawling with hired killers, and two drifters are considered expendable. But these old-timers have an ace in the hole — their friend Wild Bill Hickok has their backs . . .

WALT KEENE

DEAD MAN DRAW

Complete and Unabridged

LINFORD
Leicester

First published in Great Britain in 2014 by
Robert Hale Limited
London

First Linford Edition
published 2017
by arrangement with
Robert Hale
an imprint of The Crowood Press
Wiltshire

A catalogue record for this book is available
from the British Library.

ISBN 978–1–4448–3450–5

Published by
F. A. Thorpe (Publishing)
Anstey, Leicestershire

Set by Words & Graphics Ltd.
Anstey, Leicestershire
Printed and bound in Great Britain by
T. J. International Ltd., Padstow, Cornwall

This book is printed on acid-free paper

To the Royal Literary Fund.
With gratitude and thanks.

Prologue

Dust rose up from the horse's hoofs and hung in the cool forest air as the rider steered his mount ever upward toward the blue sky which could be seen through the dense canopy. There seemed to be no other sound within the forest apart from that which the rider was creating. He spurred and forced his elegant stallion higher into the dense mountains as if he was trying to flee the guns of his enemies yet there was no one following this rider.

The heavily armed horseman was far from the hunted. He was the hunter.

More dust drifted down between the countless trees as the horseman pulled his long leathers toward his vest and stopped the mount.

For what seemed like a lifetime the rider sat astride his mount and held the tall animal in check. Every instinct within him listened for the merest hint of where his chosen prey might have secreted himself.

No matter how hard he listened there were no sounds anywhere within the confines of the dense forest. Flint Conrad swung the horse around and began to doubt that there was any living creature within the range of his .45.

Conrad rested the palm of his hand upon the grip of his holstered weapon as he vainly strained to hear or see anything alive. Something was wrong.

Very wrong indeed.

Like a merciless creature created in the bowels of Hell his eyes darted to every leaf upon every tree or bush. He was intent on killing and yet there was nothing to even aim his gun at.

He moved his head from side to side in search of the man he had spent weeks hunting. There was no sign of anyone or anything and yet he still did not believe it.

There had to be some sign of the man he sought.

Nothing could vanish into thin air.

Conrad glanced at the dirt which led up through the trees and shook his head. The tracks had evaporated. For weeks he had trailed the distinctive hoof tracks and now they were nowhere to be found.

He rubbed his jaw.

His eyes probed the forest. The brush was thin. Too thin for anyone to hide behind. The trees were everywhere but even they could not conceal a horseman.

Where was he?

Conrad removed his Stetson and ran his fingers through his sleek black hair. An overwhelming dread filled the black-hearted soul of the hunter.

Every fibre in his body told him that something was watching his every movement and had been doing so since he first entered the vast land of trees.

There was something very different about this unholy place and yet he could not fathom what. In all his days as a hired gun he had encountered many things but nothing quite as eerie as this.

It was as though a thousand eyes were watching him but not one could be seen from where he sat atop his high-shouldered stallion.

The venomous intruder knew that he had trailed his prey to this very spot and yet now he sat staring at nothing but trees and air.

Conrad tapped his spurs and continued riding up the winding trail toward the broken rays of the noonday sunlight which filtered down through the dense canopy above him. The one thing which gnawed at the rider's craw was that no matter how far he rode into this strange forest he could not hear any hint of life.

It seemed that not one bird or critter dared break the silence for fear of the consequences. He wondered if it was the man he hunted they feared or was it him? Either way Conrad was beginning to become anxious.

Most men might have considered the odds were against him ever getting to grips with the man he chased. They might have even quit trying and turned back, but not Flint Conrad.

He had a good reason to keep hunting his prey. A thousand very good reasons. That was what he had been paid to hunt the man he was trailing: $1,000.

It did not matter to Conrad that there was no bounty on the head he hunted. The law might not want him dead but there was someone who did and Conrad had taken his money.

Conrad steadied his stallion and stood high in his stirrups. The forest had a million shadows and he knew that the rider he sought had to be within one of them.

All he had to do was find the right one and then he would find his target.

Conrad wanted to collect his blood money.

Nothing else mattered.

He sat back down and steadied his mount. A quick lash of his long leathers and the stallion started back up the steep trail. He navigated through the trees and watched the ground ahead of his horse.

Where were the tracks?

Light filtered down from the gaps in the leafy canopy and lit up the forest. Yet no matter how bright it became it still refused to betray the rider he had followed to this unholy place.

Conrad spurred. His horse gathered pace. It closed the distance between itself and the crest of the high rise. The trees thinned out as the stallion made its way toward the highest point in the uncharted land.

There was nothing but silence to greet his arrival.

The horseman drew rein and stopped his mount at the highest point in the forest. Conrad swung the horse full circle but all he could see was more trees.

Millions of them.

Suddenly a voice rang out in the clearing.

'You looking for me?' The cold, calculated words drilled into Conrad as he turned his mount and saw the man he had been hunting. 'Well, I'm here.'

Conrad held the stallion in check as it snorted like a raging bull beneath his saddle. His eyes narrowed in the sunlight and stared across the clearing at the familiar figure sitting astride his own tall mount.

Although Conrad had never set eyes upon him before there was no mistaking the figure. He had seen his likeness on the covers of countless dime novels.

The flat-brimmed Stetson hid the hooded eyes. The pale-skinned face and the moustache which concealed his mouth from view. The mane of long brown hair which settled on his wide shoulders. The fancy fringed buckskin jacket held together by the hand-tooled belt and the gleaming pearl-handled gun grips set in specially designed holsters. Holsters which were meant for an expert of the cross draw.

There was no mistaking Wild Bill Hickok.

Conrad felt the hairs of the nape of

his neck start to rise under his bandanna as he stared at his opponent.

'Why are you following me?' Hickok asked slowly.

'I've bin hired to kill you, Wild Bill,' Conrad drawled.

Hickok might have been smiling. There was no way of knowing for sure. He lowered his head and stared at the venomous hired killer and released his grip on his reins.

'Who hired you?' Hickok questioned.

Conrad inhaled deeply. 'That's my business.'

Hickok flexed his long fingers as though he were about to snatch up a poker pot rather than his guns. Without a hint of emotion the infamous figure repeated his question.

'I'll ask you again. Who hired you to kill me?'

Conrad spat and raised his gun hand.

'Somebody that don't want you living any longer, Bill.'

'Wrong answer.' Hickok snorted angrily.

Conrad went for his gun but to his utter amazement he saw something that he had never witnessed before. He saw someone who was even faster than himself. Conrad watched in total horror as he saw Hickok pull his .45s from their holsters at incredible speed.

Before the hired gunman had even cleared his holster Hickok had drawn, cocked and fired. The two deafening blasts rocked the clearing as red-hot tapers spewed from his gun barrels.

The first bullet hit Conrad high in his chest. The second punched him clean off his saddle. He rolled over his cantle and hit the ground hard.

Hickok tapped his spurs and allowed his tall elegant horse to walk across the clearing toward the prostrate figure on the ground. As he closed in on the wounded Conrad, Hickok cocked his hammers once more and trained them on the bloody remnants of what was left of the once infamous figure.

Few men could steer their horses without even holding their reins but

Hickok could. He sat astride the tall horse and stared down at Conrad. Smoke billowed from the barrels of his primed weaponry but he knew that his brief duel was over.

The horse stopped above Conrad.

Hickok blew down the barrels of his smoking guns thoughtfully. He released the hammers and showed no emotion as he slid both guns into their respective holsters.

'Who wants me dead?' he repeated. 'Give me the name of the varmint that hired you.'

Conrad stared up through the clouds of death which were smothering him. He forced a defiant smile as blood trailed from the corner of his mouth.

'You'll never know, Wild Bill.' Conrad coughed. 'But he'll not quit sending gunmen until you're dead. I might have failed but there are plenty who won't.'

Hickok gathered up his reins.

'So you ain't telling, huh?'

'I'll never tell you nothing,' Conrad choked.

Hickok poked a cigar into his mouth and watched as Conrad drowned in his own blood. He then slapped the long leathers and tapped his spurs again. The tall horse continued on down the slope.

'I'll surely find out, though,' he vowed. 'You can bet on it.'

1

Dead Man Draw was one of the largest towns in the territory and it had prospered while so many of its contemporaries had returned to dried dust. Yet like so many towns in territories which had yet to become states it was ruled by a lawless breed of men. They hired men to wear tin stars but most of those who became star packers in the wild terrain were little more than figureheads.

The real power in Dead Man Draw lay in the hands of a handful of wealthy businessmen. They called the shots and the star packers did as they were told.

Yet even in the wildest regions of what was regarded by most to be the Wild West there were some who wanted to be part of something larger. Something more civilized. Somewhere which could fly the stars and stripes and know that they had the same kind of

13

protection that the other states had.

These men were the minority, for the lawless ruled Dead Man Draw. They ruled by only one law and that was the law of the gun. Everything within the sprawling settlement was governed by an even smaller minority.

The last thing any of these wealthy businessmen desired was to have anything which remotely resembled real law and order within their town boundaries.

Early on the seventh day of the month Sheriff Jake Davis stepped out from his office with his deputy beside him. The two men walked down the long main street toward one of the town's numerous saloons.

Davis had been ordered by his paymaster to ensure he collected ten per cent from every business in Dead Man Draw and bring it to his employer.

It had started out as a quiet day.

It was business as usual as far as the two lawmen were concerned as they stepped out of the blazing sunlight and into the shadows of the saloon's porch overhang.

They had visited the Longbow Saloon many times without there being any trouble. They had collected their protection money and returned to their employer.

This day would be different.

Davis and his deputy pushed the swing doors apart and walked across the floor. Their boots parted the thick sawdust with each stride as they made their way toward the long bar set behind a string of spittoons.

There was no law in the town of Dead Man Draw.

All the town could boast was layers of rancid corruption and a few men who had controlled it for more years than any of them could recall.

Neither of the men who wore the tin stars had expected anything except gold coin when they reached the bartender at the long counter. The last thing they had imagined was that there would be another crooked man waiting for them.

A man with his mind set on taking over the lucrative business of collecting ten per cent.

Jody Walker stepped out from the darkest corner of the Longbow with both his guns cocked and drawn. He had moved toward the two lawmen swiftly.

There had been no warning.

The two star packers had expected gold.

All they got was hot lead.

Before the gunsmoke had cleared Walker had taken the small leather bag filled with golden eagles and marched out into the sunlight.

There was now another man in Dead Man Draw who regarded himself above any law conceived in the hearts and minds of good people.

Jody Walker would not stop with ten per cent of just the Longbow Saloon. There were as many saloons in town as there were trees on the surrounding hillsides.

Walker stopped and glanced at the

large, stone-block building and the three men who watched him from the second-storey window.

For the first time since the town had been built in the lawless territory Boris Day, Lucas Smart and Stu Rogers had a rival.

Jody Walker touched his hat brim at them and continued on toward the next collection. He had no fear of the trio of corrupt businessmen. They were old and fat and had relied upon Davis and his deputy to do their fighting for them.

Suddenly things had changed.

The lawmen were dead.

The sound of Walker's deadly shots still echoed around the town and the three wealthy men knew they had to do something fast if they were to maintain control of the town.

'Who is that?' Day asked his two partners in crime.

'I've never seen him before,' Rogers replied as he stared down at the man with smoke trailing from his holstered guns.

Smart poured himself a whiskey and downed it in one swallow.

'Whoever he is he's just made the biggest mistake of his life,' he snarled as he poured another shot into his glass. 'We have got to hire someone to kill him before knowledge of what he's done spreads through the territory.'

'Lucas is right,' Day nodded. 'We can't let a loose gun take control of our interests. If we do it'll be the end of us.'

Smart looked down and watched Walker enter another saloon. He swung on his heels and moved to his partners.

'We have to hire new star packers as soon as possible.'

The three men were in agreement.

2

The sound of the two deadly shots had spread like a wildfire from the town and up into the tree-covered hills. It was the reason the two drifters turned their mounts toward the distinctive sound and spurred.

Tom Dix had once been a gunfighter and even though he was now grey and long past his heyday he was still a formidable man with his guns. He rode with his old friend Dan Shaw, a man who had held every position as a lawman there was before he had retired and decided to tag along with Dix.

The horsemen cut through the line of trees and raced down the hills to where they had heard the two shots ring out. Both veteran riders were drawn like moths to a flame to where they had heard the gunfire. Neither was willing to shy away from danger.

A million trees blocked any clear view of what lay ahead as the riders drove their mounts down to where the sound of the bullets still lingered in the afternoon air. The trail led to a fast-flowing creek which cut across the paths of the saddle horses.

Dix was first to stand in his stirrups and slow his mount as he saw the crystal-clear water. Dan slowed his mount and watched his pal rein in hard.

Although the forest was dense with undergrowth the two riders felt uneasy as they approached the water. Something told Tom Dix and his saddle pal Dan Shaw they were not alone. They drew rein and dismounted as their horses reached the fast-flowing creek. The two veteran drifters held on to their reins and allowed the horses to drink as they looked out for potential trouble.

'Where do you figure them shots came from, Dixie?' Dan asked as he watched his mount drop its head and start drinking.

Dix rested against the saddle of his horse as the sun tried vainly to find a route through the trees.

'I reckon it must have come from down yonder, Dan,' Dix said as he listened to both their mounts filling their bellies.

Dan looked down the trail. 'Down there?'

'Yep.' Dix nodded slowly. 'If my eyes ain't playing tricks with me I reckon I can see chimney smoke.'

Dan Shaw moved between their horses and squinted.

'Damn it all, you're right. There are houses just beyond the trees, Dixie,' he gasped.

'I know.' Dix was far less excitable than the retired marshal. 'If you sniff the air you can tell there must be a town down there as well.'

Dan moved between their mounts and looked over the saddle at his friend.

'How come you know all that?' he

asked his pal. 'You got your eyes shut tight.'

Dix opened his eyes. 'Every town got itself a stink, Dan. I can smell a pretty strong perfume coming from a livery. A man don't have to open his eyes to smell a busy livery.'

He studied the terrain like a watchful eagle. If anything even moved out in the forest his hands moved toward his guns.

Dan looked at Dix and sucked the last of the smoke from his twisted cigarette before dropping it on to the ground and crushing it beneath his boot.

'Do you figure them shots were fired in anger, Dixie?' Dan asked as the smoke drifted back from his mouth.

Dix turned and looked over his saddle.

'What in tarnation are you talking about, Dan?' he asked. 'How in tarnation am I meant to know that? All we know for sure is that two shots rang out. The only way we'll know for sure is to go down into the town.'

Dan sighed heavily. 'I figured as much.'

Dix lifted his weary shoulders away from his drinking horse and removed his Stetson from his grey hair. He beat the dust from it against his pants leg and then returned the battered hat.

'I don't reckon we'll ride into trouble,' Dix said. 'If there was trouble I'd imagine we'd hear us a lot more shooting.'

Dan looked relieved. 'You're right, Dixie. Two shots could have just bin a drunkard letting off steam.'

'That's right,' Dix said in a soothing drawl. 'No need to get all fired up.'

'What's the name of this town?' Dan wondered. 'I never heard of any towns out here.'

Dix grinned. 'Damned if I know. We'll find out soon enough, though.'

Both men turned and stared down through the brush. The forest did lead straight to the outskirts to a town just as Dix had said. From where they were standing they could just make out the first of its buildings.

Dan scratched his chin thoughtfully as he toyed with the reins in his hands.

'I sure hope the folks there are friendly, Dixie,' Dan said as he grabbed the mane of his mount and hauled himself back up on to the saddle. 'I'm too tuckered to start fighting with strangers.'

Dix smiled even wider. 'That's old age, Dan. When you had colour you would have started a fight just to ease the boredom.'

Dan smiled as he recalled the days when they were young and relished a good fight.

'Those were the days.'

Dix checked his cinch strap and then rested a gloved hand on his saddle horn.

'You mean you can still remember them days, Dan?' he joked. 'All I can recall is the gals I used to have to beat off my handsome young body.'

'That's old age talking, Dixie,' Dan laughed. 'If nothing else, we might find us some nice fresh vittles there, old friend.'

Dix poked his boot toe into his stirrup and lifted himself up. He swung his right leg over the cantle and rammed it into the other stirrup.

'I am a tad hungry now you mention it.'

Dan slapped his reins and urged his horse through the creek with his pal close behind. They gathered pace and started to see more of the settlement as they rode closer.

It was far bigger than they had first imagined. Even the houses on the outskirts of town were plentiful. Dix drew level with his partner and looked across at his fellow rider.

'I never figured there were any big towns in this territory, Dan,' Dix said. 'Where the hell have we ended up?'

Dan Shaw held his reins in his hands as his eyes glanced all around them. Then as they rounded a large clump of trees they got the answer to their question.

A wooden marker greeted them. They both stopped their horses and studied the marker.

'Dead Man Draw,' Dix read.

Dan flicked the safety loop off his gun hammer.

'Don't sound too friendly, Dixie.'

Dix nodded in agreement.

Both riders slapped leather and urged their horses on again. They rode between the scattered buildings and continued on into the heart of the town.

3

Every one of the town's inhabitants watched as the two veteran riders allowed their mounts to trot down the middle of the long main street. Both riders were nervously aware that their arrival in Dead Man Draw was drawing so much attention.

'I reckon they don't get too many strangers in this town, Dixie,' Dan commented as they slowed their mounts.

Dix glanced all around the wide street. Every eye was looking at them as though wondering how long either of them might last.

'They sure got plenty of saloons in this town,' Dix noted as he gripped the reins of his mount tightly.

'That ain't always a good thing,' Dan added.

Dix nodded. 'You might just be right.'

The two horsemen brought their mounts to a stop outside a café. The aroma of bacon frying filled their nostrils and reminded them that they were hungry.

Dix slowly looped a leg over his cantle and lowered himself to the ground. He led his horse to a hitching rail and tied his long leathers around its twisted length. Dix surveyed the area as Dan dismounted.

'That bacon sure smells mighty fine,' Dan commented.

Dix stepped up on to the boardwalk and gave the street another glance. He did not turn until he heard his pal twist the door handle of the café.

'You coming in, Dixie?' Dan asked as he paused in the jar of the door.

Dix swung on his heels and followed his friend into the small café. He closed the door and removed his hat as Dan found an empty table close to the window. The light from the oil lamp inside the café spilled out through the window on to the street.

He dropped his hat on an empty chair and sat down. Besides them every table within the confines of the small café was empty.

'The grub sure smells good,' Dan said as he leaned back and inhaled the aroma. 'I sure could use some hot vittles in my belly. I'm darn sick of jerky.'

Dix sat and stared out of the window. 'Sure does smell good, Dan.'

Dan removed his own hat and dropped it next to his partner's Stetson.

'What's so damn interesting out there, Dixie?' he asked.

Dix glanced at Dan. 'I'm just looking.'

'What you looking for, Dixie?' Dan asked as he saw a well-rounded female emerge from the back room and start to approach them.

Dix smiled. 'You know me. I'm kinda fretful.'

'You worry too much,' Dan said.

The female stopped above them. 'What'll it be, boys?'

'Bacon and eggs, ma'am,' Dan replied from behind a large smile. 'And a pot of coffee.'

She looked at Dix. 'And what do you want?'

Dix looked up at the female. She was handsome. He smiled even wider than his pal.

'I'll have the same, ma'am.'

She nodded. 'It won't be long.'

'Thank you kindly.' Dix smiled as he noticed she was swaying her ample hips as she made her way back to the back room.

Dan pulled out his tobacco pouch. He started to sprinkle the fine tobacco on to his gummed paper and eyed his partner carefully. He ran his tongue along the gummed edge of the paper and then placed the cigarette between his lips.

Finally their eyes met across the checked tablecloth as Dan struck a match and cupped its flame. They both laughed.

'Careful you don't make no promises

your body can't keep, Dixie,' Dan said through a cloud of smoke. 'She's a mighty strong-looking gal.'

'I was just looking, Dan,' Dix laughed.

There had been others who were also looking. Looking at the arrival of two strangers in the midst of Dead Man Draw. These were not the countless townspeople but the three businessmen in their granite offices.

Day nursed his whiskey before downing it in one swallow. He had been the first of the three to spot the two riders as they entered the remote town. He walked back to where the cut-glass decanters rested and placed his empty tumbler down.

'Well? Did any of you have the same idea as me?' Day asked as he poured another two fingers of the amber liquor into his glass.

Smart was still staring through the window down across the street at the café and the two strangers who were seated near the café window.

'They're kinda old, Boris,' Smart noted.

'They can't be that old, Lucas,' Day said. 'They're drifters and a man has to be pretty fit to spend most of the time riding.'

Rogers walked to where Day stood. He filled his own glass with whiskey and turned to the older man.

'I think you might have an idea brewing in that mind of yours, Boris.' He smiled knowingly. 'We need us two new lawmen to do our dirty work for us.'

Day lifted his glass to his lips. He paused.

'And those two look mighty capable.'

Smart walked to the others. He frowned and snatched up the decanter and filled his own glass to the brim. He downed its contents and then pulled a silver cigar case from his inside jacket pocket.

'Can you be sure they're up to it?' he asked. 'They might get themselves shot down the first time they try to collect our dues. Then there's that varmint Jody Walker who killed Davis and his deputy. He might decide they have to be killed as well.'

Boris Day took a mouthful of whiskey and then looked straight at Rogers. A cruel smile etched his face.

'Who'll give a damn if they do get themselves killed?' he asked Smart. 'We can always hire someone equally as dumb as they are.'

The three men all laughed as they considered their plan.

Smart dropped down into a well-padded leather chair and crossed his legs. He struck a match and lit his fat cigar.

'You're right. Who'll give a damn?'

The office rocked with laughter.

4

The sun was slowly sinking in the blue, cloudless sky. Long shadows stretched from one side of the street to the other as the two veteran drifters left the warmth of the café and stood on the boardwalk. Dix rested a hip on the hitching rail as Dan gave out a satisfied yawn and stepped down on to the sand and pulled his reins free.

'Where do you reckon we're gonna find us a bed for the night, Dixie?' Dan asked as he toyed with his reins.

Dix was about to suggest they locate a hotel when a youth of no more than fifteen hailed them from the doorway of the large, stone-block building.

Dix stepped down next to Dan and pointed at the youngster who was heading toward them.

'Is he whistling at us?' Dan queried.

Dix shrugged. 'I don't know why but I reckon he is.'

'I hate whistling,' Dan sighed.

The youngster stopped beside the two drifters. He looked them up and down as if he did not believe he had found the right two men. He turned and looked up to the window where the three businessmen were watching. They nodded and the youngster turned to face Dix and Dan again.

'My bosses wanna know if you've got a job?' the kid asked.

Dix stepped forward.

'First things first, son. What's your name?'

The youth looked dumbfounded. He scratched his mop of ginger hair and answered.

'My name's Toby.'

Dan rested a hand on the youngster's shoulder. 'Now what's so important, Toby?'

'Like I just told you,' Toby said. 'My bosses want to give you a job.'

Dix raised an eyebrow. 'Your bosses

want to hire us?'

'They sure do.' Toby shrugged in surprise. 'Damned if I know why. There sure are a lot of younger folks in town to give jobs to. I can't think why they'd wanna hire you two old-timers.'

Dix gave out a loud laugh.

Dan shook his head. 'This kid don't even know when he's insulting folks.'

'Who are your bosses, Toby?' Dix asked.

The lad turned and pointed up at the high window. 'They're up there. Mr Day, Mr Smart and Mr Rogers.'

Dan patted the boy on the shoulder. 'Thank you kindly for bringing us the message, Toby. Now high-tail it before this old-timer kicks your butt.'

The youth ran around the two men and entered the café behind them. Both Dix and Dan stared across at the building to the high window Toby had pointed at. They saw the three men back away from the window.

Dix kicked at the dust. 'Something tells me this ain't all it seems, pard.'

'I know what you mean. You hankering for a job, Dixie?' Dan asked.

'If I wasn't down to my last five bucks I'd say no.'

'C'mon,' Dan said. 'We're too broke to be picky.'

The two drifters led their mounts across the wide street to the large stone building. Both men looped their leathers over the pole and looked at the massive building bathed in the light of the setting sun. There were no signs to indicate what the huge structure was but every one of the townsfolk knew exactly what it was.

It was the very heart of Dead Man Draw.

This was where the three most powerful men in town ruled the roost from. This was their power base. The place where three corrupt souls ruled over so many others. They did not require the law of so many other towns in the west. They used gun law to achieve their goals.

Dix pushed his hat off his brow and

stared up at the solid building. He rubbed his whiskered jaw thoughtfully.

'What are you thinking about, Dixie?' Dan asked as he stepped up beside his pal.

'I'm just wondering who that kid's bosses are,' Dix replied thoughtfully. 'I don't cotton to being hired by some bunch of crooks.'

Dan smiled. 'I'd not start fretting too soon. Once they see us I reckon they'll change their minds about giving us any work.'

Dixie led the way up the steps to the large door. He entered with his partner close at his side. It was far cooler inside the stone walls of the building. A wide staircase stood before them. They had heard tales of such grand buildings but had never actually seen one before.

'Must have taken ten trees to make that staircase, Dan,' Dix noted.

Dan nodded. 'Didn't make much of a dent in that forest we just spent three weeks riding through, Dixie.'

They were about to venture forward

when they realized that two large men had appeared to either side of them. Dix glanced to both sides as the men gestured to the staircase.

'Reckon we're meant to walk up them steps, Dan,' Dix said as he rested his wrists on his guns.

'Damn it all,' Dan sighed. 'My old bones ain't designed for climbing.'

They both walked to the stairs and began to walk up toward a large window. Dix kept his hands resting on his holstered gun grips as they listened to the echoes of their steps.

There was something haunting about the huge building. It seemed totally out of place in a town of mainly wooden structures. The two men reached the landing and paused as Dan rubbed his knees whilst Dix surveyed what lay around them.

Suddenly a voice echoed from one of the many rooms. It drew both of their attention.

Dix was first to face the voice and stare at the rotund figure of Boris Day as he stood near a ten-foot-high door.

'Will you please come this way, gentlemen?'

Dan straightened up and trailed Dix across the gleaming floor of the landing toward the large man.

Day stepped aside and waved them into the room. Dix entered first and nodded at Smart and Rogers who were standing beside the windows.

'Take a seat, gentlemen,' Day said as he moved to a desk and sat himself down. 'My name's Boris Day. These are my associates, Lucas Smart and Stu Rogers.'

Dix lowered himself down on to a leather chair and touched his hat brim.

'Howdy, folks.'

Dan remained standing. 'What's all this about?'

Boris Day smiled. It was a sickly smile which neither Dix nor Dan cared for.

'We run Dead Man Draw,' Day said as he picked a half-smoked cigar up from an ashtray and placed it between his teeth. 'We are looking for two men to fill the post of sheriff and deputy. We would like to offer you the positions.'

'You would?' Dix touched his ear lobe.

Dan looked down at Dix and then returned his eyes to the seated man behind the desk.

'We're both obliged but kinda curious,' Dan remarked.

'Curious?' Day repeated the word. 'Why would you be curious? I'd have thought that you would be flattered and perhaps even a tad grateful.'

Dix narrowed his eyes as they darted between the three men in the room. There was something that he did not like about them.

'Me and Dan heard shots as we approached Dead Man Draw,' Dix said quietly. 'I got me a gut feeling that's why there happens to be two job vacancies. Am I right?'

Rogers walked toward the seated Dix. He stared angrily down at the veteran gunfighter.

'Do you want the jobs or not?' he snapped.

Dix stood and faced Rogers. 'Sure we want the jobs. Me and Dan ain't work-shy. I'm just wondering why you've offered them to us.'

'We're strangers in town,' Dan added. 'It just seems a little odd that you've offered the jobs to two strangers when you've a town full of men.'

Day raised a hand to silence his partner.

'You are both correct. The two shots you heard did cut down our previous two law officers.' Day sighed as he lit his cigar and drew in its smoke. 'The trouble is that everyone in Dead Man Draw knows one another and that ain't good for business. We always like to hire outsiders to work as lawmen.'

'And you own this town,' Dix said.

'We control it,' Day said through a cloud of smoke.

'I figured that,' Dix nodded.

Dan turned back to face Day. 'I'm a retired lawman so I've a lot of experience. You didn't know it but you have chosen the right men for the job.'

Both Rogers and Smart moved to the desk. They leaned over the ink blotter and whispered to their partner. Finally the men separated from their huddle and faced Dan and Dix.

'I'm pleased that our judgement has proved to be so vital, gentlemen,' Day said. 'Now, what are your names?'

Dan watched as Day dipped a pen into an ink-well and hovered its nib over a sheet of paper.

'My name's Dan Shaw,' he said.

Day scribbled the name and then looked up at Dix. 'And what do they call you, my friend?'

'Tom Dix.'

When Day had finished writing he placed the pen back into its holder. He smiled again.

'The pay is $200 a month each,' he said, before adding, 'plus a percentage of all you collect.'

Dix moved closer to the desk and looked down at the man with the cigar gripped between his teeth.

'Collect? What exactly are we meant to collect, Day?'

'Your main duties will be collecting money from all of the businesses in town.' Day tapped the ash from his cigar and looked up at the two drifters before him. 'This is a peaceful town and you will make sure it stays that way.'

Dix rested his gloved hands on the desk and glared down at the rotund figure.

'Are you telling us that we'll be collecting your protection money?'

'Exactly.'

Dix straightened up and looked at Dan.

'What do you reckon, Dan?'

Dan raised an eyebrow. 'I was a lawman for an awful long while, Dixie. Sometimes I had to collect weekly dues from businesses. Mainly it was for town councils. Sort of like taxes.'

Dix tilted his head and started to nod.

'If you reckon it's OK then I guess it is.' He shrugged.

Boris Day stood. 'So you are agreeable?'

'We'll sign on for a couple of months,' Dan said.

Dix rubbed his chin. 'When's payday? I need a shave.'

Rogers stepped forward and handed both men a twenty-dollar bill. 'That's a bonus on top of your wages.'

Smart handed Dan a sheet of paper. 'And this is a list of your duties. It tells you which businesses you have to collect from.'

Boris Day walked around his desk and pinned the sheriff star on Dan's vest and then went to pin the deputy star on to Dix's shirt front.

Tom Dix rested his hands on his guns and looked down at the gleaming star. His eyes flashed up at Day and then he stepped closer to the big man.

'You forgot something,' Dix told him. 'You forgot something real important.'

Day pulled his cigar from his mouth.

'What have we forgotten, Dix?'

Dan looked at his pal curiously.

'Yeah, what has he forgotten to tell us, Dixie?'

'He's forgotten to tell us the name of the hombre that killed their last sheriff and deputy,' Dix retorted. 'I got me a feeling that varmint is mighty dangerous to folks wearing tin stars.'

5

Tom Dix left the building beside his friend and both made their way down to their awaiting mounts. Neither was happy at the prospect of working as glorified money collectors but they resolved that they had no option. Dix pulled his reins from the hitching pole and held them in his hands as he studied the long street.

Dan moved beside Dix.

'I reckon you ain't too pleased at us being hired by them folks, Dixie,' Dan sighed.

Dix gave a nod.

'I don't blame you,' Dan added as he tugged his own reins from the pole and gathered them up in his hands. 'I've got me the bitterest taste in my mouth.'

Dix turned and grabbed hold of his saddle horn. He mounted his horse and steadied it as his eyes looked down at the gleaming deputy badge pinned to his clothing.

'There's something kinda odd about all this, Dan,' he said. 'I just don't know what it is yet.'

'You're right, pal.' Dan pushed his boot into his stirrup and eased himself up on to his saddle. 'Something is kinda fishy about all this.'

Dix pulled his hat brim down. 'So we find a hotel?'

'Reckon we ought to find the sheriff's office first, Dixie,' Dan said. 'We might just find some clue to what exactly is going on in Dead Man Draw.'

Dixie raised a finger and pointed to their right.

'I saw the office when we rode into town. It's down thataway.'

Both men urged their horses on. The sound of hoofs seemed to echo off the array of structures which dominated the centre of the town. Dix led the way as a solitary figure lit one street lantern after another along the main thoroughfare. As they rode along the street both noticed that the coming of nightfall had not diminished the amount of people on the town's boardwalks.

A glowing amber light spilled out from saloons, gambling halls and the various stores which remained open for business.

'It looks like the folks around here didn't stay in mourning for long, Dixie,' Dan noted as he navigated the length of the street.

'Reckon star packers ain't valued too highly in Dead Man draw, Dan.' Dixie nodded as he drew back on his reins and steered his mount toward the small sheriff's office set between two saloons.

Both riders dismounted and led their horses up to the unlit structure. Dan tied his reins to a porch upright as Dix stepped up on the boardwalk and peered in through the windows.

'Ain't you gonna tie your horse up, Dixie?' Dan asked as he studied the busy saloons the office was crammed between.

Dix threw his reins to his pal. 'You tie him up.'

Dan caught the reins and shook his head. 'I'm the sheriff, you know.'

Dix turned and smiled. 'You tie the horse up, Sheriff.'

Before Dan could utter another word he saw Dix turn the rusted doorknob and enter the dark office.

Dix moved to a lamp and raised its glass bowl before striking a match and touching its wick. The office erupted into light as Dan walked in behind his pal.

'Ain't much of an office, Dixie.'

Dix blew out the match and lowered the glass bowl. The room grew even lighter as he adjusted the brass wheel. For a moment he did not say anything as his eyes darted around the office. The office comprised one room and two jail cells. A wall rack with two repeating rifles and a scattergun dominated the wall behind a large desk.

'I've seen a lot worse offices, Dan,' Dix said as he pulled open the desk drawers and found nothing but Wanted posters.

Dan stared at the pot-belly stove and a coffee pot sitting upon its top. A blackened chimney went up the wall and then exited out just above the window.

'Not bad I guess,' Dan admitted. 'I've worked in a lot worse.'

Dix walked back to the door and paused. He looked at Dan and then said, 'I'll take the horses to the livery stable and you can make us a pot of coffee.'

Dan glanced at his pal. 'What you want coffee for? I thought we were going to find ourselves a hotel.'

'Make the coffee, Dan,' Dix repeated. 'I'll hire us a room after I get the horses bedded down.'

Dan was about to reply when Dix closed the door and mounted his gelding. Dan stood beside the window and watched as his partner led his horse out into the street.

The stove was still alight. He opened

its door and pushed two logs into it from a kindling box. The flames grew around the bone-dry logs.

He sighed heavily. 'I reckon I'll make the coffee.'

6

The word of what Jody Walker had done earlier had raced throughout the settlement like wildfire. It had filled all of the businesses in Dead Man Draw with a fear unlike any they had ever felt before. They had grown used to handing over money to Sheriff Davis and his deputy but now they did not know what to expect.

The Broken Spur was the busiest saloon in town and as the last rays of the sun vanished from view it fell into total silence as its patrons spotted Jody Walker standing on the boardwalk looking in.

He rested a hand upon its swing doors.

Walker had only been in Dead Man Draw for three months and yet he had made his presence felt. He had already killed three men in fights with both his fists as well as his guns.

The law was always different in the territories.

Men who were good with their weaponry tended to be left alone even by those who wore tin stars. Walker had realized that this town was ripe and he had only just started to harvest its bounty.

He pushed the doors inward and entered.

His pockets were swollen with the money he had collected and yet he wanted more. Every man and woman within the Broken Spur backed away as he strode across the sawdust-covered floor toward the long bar counter.

Walker rested a boot upon the brass rail and then dropped the two large bags of money next to an empty glass. His eyes glanced at the faces of the men and bar girls. He defied any of them to utter a word.

'What'll it be, Jody?' the bartender asked.

'I want money,' Walker said. 'The

money you usually hand over to the sheriff. He's dead and don't need it no longer.'

The bartender swallowed hard. 'I'll have to get the boss, Jody. He handles the collection.'

Walker nodded and curled his finger at a bar girl. She reluctantly moved toward him.

When she was within reach he grabbed her and pulled her close. He inhaled her perfume and whispered into her ear. Her expression changed from fear to horror. She looked at the ceiling as Walker chewed on her neck. Everyone within the Broken Spur knew that the female wanted to run but none of the men dared take on the ruthless Walker.

Walker grunted with laughter as he saw the owner of the saloon leading the bartender through the crowd back toward him. He pushed the bar girl away and placed both his hands on the damp counter.

'C'mon. I ain't got all day,' Walker shouted.

Pete Mason had owned the Broken Spur for three years. As he moved behind the bar toward Walker he felt uneasy. He had grown used to the sheriff's regular visits but this felt different.

'What do you want, Walker?' Mason asked firmly.

'The collection money,' Walker spat.

Mason started to nod. 'I ain't bin told about you taking over the collection, Walker.'

A crooked smile etched the face of Jody Walker. He was breathing fast as he stretched to his full height.

'Get the collection money now.' He snarled like a rabid dog. 'There's a new set of rules in this town and I'm the critter making them rules. Savvy?'

Mason stepped back.

'It don't work like that.'

Every eye within the saloon watched as Mason reached down under the counter and dragged out a scattergun. The Broken Spur resounded with the sound of females screaming as they raced to the walls.

Walker hauled both his guns from their holsters as the scattergun was raised. He pulled hard on his triggers and sent two blinding shots into the saloon owner's chest. As Mason fell backward his lifeless finger managed to squeeze the trigger of his huge scatter-gun.

As Mason hit the floor the ceiling above them was ripped apart by the shotgun cartridge. Debris fell over the body and the grinning Walker.

The bartender raced to his dead boss and knelt beside his limp carcass. He looked up at Walker just as the merciless killer cocked his guns again.

The bartender stared into the smoking barrels of Walker's guns and began to fear that he was about to join his boss on his way to Boot Hill.

'Please don't shoot, Jody.'

'I won't if you get me the collection money,' Walker said through gritted teeth. 'Well?'

The bartender reached carefully

under the counter and picked up a bag. He placed it on the counter.

'Here it is, Jody.' He gulped nervously. 'It was here all the time.'

Walker smiled and opened the bag. He stared at the golden coins and then started to laugh.

'Much obliged,' he drawled. 'It's a pity Mason didn't recall that. He might still be alive if he had.'

7

The sound of the deadly shots rippled through the long wide street and washed over the man wearing the tin star as he stepped up on to the boardwalk and headed back toward the sheriff's office. A sudden dread filled the heart of Tom Dix as he caught the scent of brewing coffee just ahead of him. Dix feared that the man that had killed the previous lawmen might have decided to send Dan on his way to meet his Maker as well. The ancient gunfighter began to run along Main Street toward the office. A crowd of people from the saloons had gathered on the boardwalks to either side of the small office. Dix forced his way through the crowd to the office.

To his relief the shooting had come from somewhere else within Dead Man Draw. He stopped and breathlessly stared down through the amber illumination.

Dan opened the office door and stepped out on to the boardwalk. He glanced at Dix.

'Two more shots,' Dan muttered.

Dix nodded. 'Yep, two more shots.'

The patrons of the saloons soon got bored and filtered back into their favoured drinking holes. Within seconds only the two men wearing the tin stars remained.

'I made the coffee, Dixie,' Dan said.

Dix continued to stare through the amber light down toward the distant buildings. He did not reply.

Dan went to walk back into the office when his partner's gloved hand gripped his arm. Dan looked over his shoulder at Dix.

'The coffee can wait, Dan,' Dix said.

'What do you reckon on doing?' Dan asked. 'It might just be some drunken hotheads letting off steam. The shooting has stopped after all.'

Dix was not so easily convinced.

'Maybe, but I sure doubt it.'

Dan looked at the face of his friend. A face which time had not been gentle with. He knew that Dix had an instinct for trouble. He had honed it since he was a hired gunfighter and it was usually right.

'I know that look you're wearing,' Dan said. 'It usually means there's trouble and you got a habit of dragging us both into it. What do you figure we oughta do, Dixie?'

Dix raised an eyebrow.

'We're wearing stars, ain't we?'

Dan gave a nod and pulled the office door shut behind him and frowned. 'Damn it all. Here we go again.'

Both men started back along the street to where they felt the gunshots had originated. They moved swiftly through the eerie street illumination. The light of glowing lanterns spilled down in pools around the base of each of their poles and was only matched by the light of the saloons and storefronts.

A score of shadows stretched out from the buildings.

Dix was first to be aware that the street was no longer busy. It was now empty of all living souls apart from a scattering of saddle horses tied up outside the many saloons and whore-houses.

'I don't like this, Dan,' Dix admitted as he pulled the leather safety loops off his gun hammers. 'This is a mighty good place to get bushwhacked.'

Dan looked all around them as they continued to make their way along the deserted thoroughfare. He glanced at every black shadow nervously.

'Now you come to mention it there sure are a lot of places a back-shooter might hide himself in, Dixie,' he noted. 'Whoever fired them shots might be waiting in any of these damn shadows. Waiting for a couple of *hombres* with tin stars pinned to their chests to use as targets.'

Dix moved his arm and stopped Dan in his tracks.

'What you seen, Dixie?' Dan whispered as his hand rested on his holstered gun grip.

'Look up there.' Dix pointed at the Broken Spur. Its light cascaded out from its windows and door. It lit up the sand and nearly reached the massive stone-block building opposite.

Dan sighed. 'That's just a saloon.'

Dix nodded and led his companion up under a porch. He rested a shoulder against its wall and kept his eyes fixed upon the Broken Spur.

'Don't that strike you as being mighty odd, Dan?'

Dan looked confused.

'Nope.' He sighed heavily. 'That's just a damn saloon. This town is full of the things or ain't you noticed?'

'I noticed all the other saloons,' Dix said as he drew one of his guns from its holster and cocked its hammer. 'But didn't you notice how noisy they all are?'

Dan was about to speak when he realized what his pal meant. He rested a hand on Dix's shoulder.

'You're right,' he said. 'And that saloon is all lit up and as quiet as the grave. What's it mean, Dixie?'

Dix raised his gun and rested it against the porch upright as he studied The Broken Spur. He did not know the answer but he intended to find out. He looked back at his friend.

'C'mon, Dan. Let's go get us a drink.'

Dan shook his head wearily and followed.

Dix moved like a man half his age through the shadows of the closed and shuttered stores. He used each shadow to his advantage as they slowly drew closer to their goal.

They both rested when they reached the corner of the saloon. Dix tilted his head. He still could not hear a sound coming from within The Broken Spur. Dan edged closer.

'How come the saloon is so quiet, Dixie?' Dan asked. 'It ain't natural for a saloon to be as quiet as this one is.'

Dix signalled for his pal to follow him up on to the boardwalk toward the lamplight. The two men moved like phantoms to the swing doors and paused when they reached their objective.

Dix leaned out and looked into the saloon.

'What you see, Dixie?' Dan whispered.

'Something real strange,' Dix answered and placed his free hand on top of the swing doors. He pushed them inward and entered.

The swing doors rocked on their hinges as Dix and Dan stood facing the crowd of silent people. Dix held his gun at hip height as his eyes darted from one face to another.

Dix had never seen so many people in a saloon who looked so utterly terrified before. Yet he knew that it was neither he nor Dan that these people were frightened of.

Dan moved closer to his pal and spoke into Dix's ear.

'What in tarnation's wrong with these folks, Dixie? They look like they just seen a ghost.'

'Maybe they've seen something a lot more dangerous than ghosts, Dan,' Dix said and marched across the saloon toward the bar counter. He stopped and then looked at the faces of the people who were gathered against the far wall.

Dan reached the bar a few heartbeats after his friend.

'This is sure the quietest saloon I've ever bin in, Dixie,' he commented. 'I don't get it.'

Dix nudged his pal.

'I do.' Dix looked over the bar counter and pointed.

'What the hell?' Dan gasped at the sight of Pete Mason's body. The two neat bullet holes in his chest were masked by the blood.

Dix turned and rested his back against the mahogany counter top.

'Looks like we found an answer to the shots we heard.' Dix looked at one of the bar girls and stepped toward her. She was terrified but stood her ground.

'What you want?' she asked Dix.

'Who did this?' Dix asked.

'Jody Walker,' she sighed.

'Is he gone?'

She nodded.

'He's gone for now.'

Dix tilted and looked down at the petite female.

'What else, ma'am?' he asked her.

'Walker's got himself a bunch of stinking friends just as loco as he is, Deputy. Walker was alone tonight but I got me a feeling that when he rounds up his pals they'll be back.'

'Why'd he come here and kill that man?' Dix asked.

'He wanted the collection money,' she informed him. 'That's why he killed Sheriff Davis and his deputy earlier. They were collecting the monthly dues of all the businesses. Walker must have decided he'd collect all the money for himself.'

'That's mighty interesting,' Dix said. She looked into his eyes.

'Listen up, Deputy,' she warned. 'Walker has already killed two men wearing tin stars and I've a feeling he won't quit when he learns there are two more in town.'

'Much obliged, ma'am.' Dix touched the brim of his hat and then turned back toward Dan. He bit his lip and slid his gun back into its holster.

'I got me a feeling that she's right,' Dix said thoughtfully. 'We're in worse danger than I first figured.'

Dan swallowed hard.

'Mr Day must have forgotten to tell us how dangerous this Walker varmint is, Dixie.'

'Looks that way. At least we know his name and what he wanted here.'

Dan shrugged. 'This Walker critter must be a maniac, Dixie. To kill like that just ain't right.'

Dix nodded and glanced around at the faces of the still-shocked people inside The Broken Spur. They were too afraid to venture out and go back to their homes.

'And that little lady reckons he's got himself friends, Dan,' Dix said.

'A gang?'

'Sounds like that.' Dix rubbed his jaw. 'C'mon, Dan.'

The silent patrons of The Broken Spur watched as the two newly appointed lawmen walked back out into the night. They were still afraid and still as quiet as church mice.

8

Jody Walker rode his beleaguered mount through the outskirts of Dead Man Draw toward a small shack. As he reached the shack Walker dismounted and pulled the swollen saddle-bags from behind his cantle. He staggered with the hefty bags filled with the small fortune he had collected from just three of the town's saloons weighing him down. He kicked the shack door open and tossed the bags on to the bare boards. Walker rested on the cot and then scratched a match across the floor and allowed its flame to ignite the tip of his cigar.

His cold-blooded eyes stared at the bags on the floor as the rays of the moon illuminated them. A triumphant grin etched his face.

He filled his lungs with smoke and then blew a long line of the grey smoke at his bloody boots. With each drag on the cigar he laughed. It had been so easy he wondered why no one else had ever decided to do it before he had.

There was not a living soul in Dead Man Draw with any guts, he thought. If there was anyone in town with a spine they would have fought him but all they had done was knuckle under. He knew that the leather saddle-bags were only just the beginning. There was no one willing or able to stop him from gathering up all of the money in town just as Day, Smart and Rogers must have done years earlier. There was only one law in Dead Man Draw and that was gun law.

Given a few days his guns would make him the richest man in town. His grin grew broader.

Suddenly he heard the sound of approaching riders.

Walker stood and drew both his guns. He moved to the window, pulled the makeshift drape from across the window and stared through the large hole in the middle of its broken glass pane into the murky night.

He watched as the two horsemen steered their mounts through the mist toward his shack. A knowing smile etched his features as he dropped both guns back into their holsters as he recognized them.

Like a panther he moved to the door, pulled it open and stepped out on to the sand. His eyes narrowed as they focused on the pair of riders.

'Howdy, boys,' Walker yelled as he waved his arms over his head. 'You two sidewinders looking for me?'

Both riders drew rein and stopped their horses at the front of the ramshackle dwelling. Duke Lee and Frank Green were cut from the same cloth as Walker himself yet they had never stooped as low as he had. They were the scum that all towns have hiding in their shadows but unlike Walker neither had ever killed anyone.

The three had been nothing but

trouble since they had first learned to talk and walk. Between them they were responsible for scores of horrific crimes in the territory and yet they had never been brought to book.

'I wondered when you two would show,' Walker bellowed.

'What you looking so smug about, Jody?' Lee asked as he looped his leg over the neck of his sorrowful mount and slid to the ground. 'You look like the cat that cornered the cream.'

Walker roared with laughter as his teeth firmly gripped on to his cigar.

'I just had me the biggest day of my entire life, Duke.'

Green dropped from his horse with a half-bottle of whiskey in his hand. He was grinning as he approached the elated Walker.

'And what would that kinda day be, Jody?' he asked.

Walker led them into the dimly lit shack. They all sat on the cot and shared a few slugs of the whiskey before Walker decided to tell them of his blood-soaked day.

'I was in town and I had me an idea.' Walker puffed on his cigar. 'I thought about them lawmen who once a month visit every damn saloon and whorehouse.'

Duke Lee nodded. 'I've seen the sheriff and his deputy collecting the dues for them three fat old men up in the big building too. So what?'

'I can think of better ways to spend a day than just watching them lawmen collecting money, Jody,' Green laughed.

Walker jumped up from the cot, picked up the saddle-bags and threw them at his pals. The sound of coins filled the shack as the bags hit the boards before the two men's feet.

Green lowered his bottle from his lips and stared at the bag. Even in the unlit shack he knew what was in the satchels of the saddle-bags.

'That's money,' he gasped.

'Damn right it is,' Walker laughed.

Lee leaned down and opened the

closest flap of the bags and squinted into it. He stared at the moonlit coins and then looked up at Walker.

'How'd you get all this money, Jody?' he asked.

Walker moved to them and puffed on his cigar. His arms were like windmills as they rotated with every word that left his lips.

'I was watching Sheriff Davis and his deputy for about an hour and then had me a real smart notion,' Walker began. 'They kept going into gambling houses and saloons and then they'd come out carrying bags full of money. They then took the money to Boris Day and his cronies. I figured that I'd kinda cut in on their square dance.'

Lee rocked with laughter.

'You mean that Davis just let you take the collection money, Jody?' Green smiled.

Walker grinned through the cigar smoke which encircled his head.

'Not exactly. I had to kill them lawmen first. Then they let me.'

Lee stood. 'You killed them?'

Green took another swig of whiskey. 'It ain't healthy killing star packers, Jody.'

'Not for them it ain't,' Walker chuckled. 'Now it's real healthy, boys. Now there ain't nobody that can stop me collecting every cent that usually ends up in the pockets of Day and his partners.'

Lee looked worried. 'You were just lucky, Jody. I'd not stretch my luck too far if I was you.'

'Luck had nothing to do with it.' Walker gave a sigh. 'After I killed them lawmen I walked into two more saloons and they just handed the loot over. Mind you I had to kill Pete Mason in The Broken Spur to convince him. After that it was plumb easy.'

Lee moved to the side of Walker.

'With that amount of money you can ride out of this town and have yourself a real good time, Jody,' he suggested. 'That's what I'd do.'

Walker shook his head.

'I ain't running away, Duke. There ain't no need.'

Green looked over the neck over his bottle. 'You figuring on staying in Dead Man Draw?'

'I sure am,' Walker announced. 'When we kill Day, Smart and Rogers we can help ourselves to what's in their safe. There ain't nobody to stop us.'

Lee nodded.

'That's right. You done killed the lawmen,' he smiled.

'There's nobody with any guts left in this entire town to stop us doing whatever we wanna do, boys,' Walker said thoughtfully before grabbing the whiskey bottle out of Green's hands. 'At daybreak we'll strike. By sundown we'll be the richest *hombres* in the territory. Are you with me?'

Green exhaled.

'You can count me in, Jody,' he said.

'I'll sure enjoy filling them three fat old men with lead, Jody,' Lee chortled.

Walker took a swig from the bottle and then returned it to Green. 'You boys can bed down here tonight. We'll get up nice and early and hit them before they've had time to wipe the sleep from their eyes.'

9

At the other end of Dead Man Draw the pair of newly appointed lawmen wrestled with the problems they could see gathering around them. There was more to the seemingly simple job of collecting money for the trio of businessmen who had hired them than they had at first imagined.

They had seen his handiwork with their own eyes. Pete Mason had been brutally cut down by the man they knew only as Walker. He posed more than a hint of danger to both Dix and Dan. They both knew from experience that when someone like Walker killed one man he would not flinch from adding to his tally.

So far he had slain three men. It was a tally that they knew would get larger. Walker had killed without anyone trying to stop him. That was like pouring coal oil on a fire.

An hour had passed since Dix and Dan had returned to the sheriff's office. It was more than enough time for their fears to multiply. The tin stars on their chests were meaningless if they simply collected money for Boris Day and his cohorts. They had to do what real lawmen always did in these situations and that meant they had to try and stop the killings.

Even if it meant risking their own necks, they had to try and stop Walker from continuing his slaughtering.

One by one the saloons and gambling halls began to close throughout Dead Man Draw. As each of the nocturnal businesses locked their doors the long street grew even darker. They had drunk half the pot of coffee and were brooding about what they ought to do next.

Dix glanced above Dan's head at the wall clock.

'It ain't even midnight yet,' he complained.

Dan blinked hard and stared across the desk at his friend and exhaled loudly.

'Did you rent us a hotel room like you was intending, Dixie?' Dan asked as he blew at the whirlpool of black beverage in the tin cup.

'Sure I did. I put the nags in the livery and then I went into the hotel and rented us a room,' Dix said. 'Just like I told you I would. Fat lot of good that room is doing us, though.'

Dan warmed his hands and sipped the black beverage. 'Our horses are having a better rest than either you or me.'

Dix rose up from the hardback chair and rubbed his aching back. He walked to the window and stared out at the street. He glanced at his partner.

'I'm tuckered, Dan. We ought to head on down to the hotel and make use of them beds,' he said. 'We sure ain't getting no place sitting in here. I reckon that Walker critter has quit killing for today.'

Dan finished his coffee and stood. He moved from behind the desk and made his way close to Dix. He looked out of the office window.

'You're right, Dixie,' he agreed. 'It seems like a real waste of money to let them hotel beds go to waste. The saloons are shutting down for the night. I agree that Walker ain't gonna do any more killing tonight.'

Dix plucked his Stetson off the hatstand and placed it on to his head of grey hair.

'So we're quitting for the night?' he asked.

'Yep. We're quitting for the night, Dixie.' Dan smiled and grabbed his own hat. 'Let's get to that hotel and get us some shuteye.'

'Now you're talking.' Dix blew out the lamp and then opened the office door. Both men walked out on to the boardwalk. Dix surveyed the street carefully. It was now quiet.

Dan slid the key into the lock and turned it.

As he placed the key into his vest pocket Dix placed a hand on his shoulder.

'You can't shake off being a lawman, can you?' Dix said. 'No matter how hard you try you're still an old star packer at heart.'

Dan nodded in agreement. 'Old habits are mighty hard to shake off, Dixie.'

They stepped down on to the sand and began to head toward the distant hotel.

The lawless settlement was getting quieter with every beat of their hearts. They moved through the moonlight toward the opposite side of Main Street.

The eerie quiet engulfed both the star packers. Neither could recall the last time they had been in a situation like the one they had somehow found themselves embroiled in. Although neither man mentioned it, they both regretted being drawn here by the sound of the two gunshots.

Dead Man Draw was like a spider's web and they were like helpless flies. No matter how hard they fought it they could not escape being tangled up.

Was Walker the spider?

Were they his prey?

Or were they just too dog-tired to think straight?

They continued on across the sand.

'I'm not as young as I once was, Dixie,' Dan said as he followed his friend's lead. 'Being a sheriff used to be easy but now I'm tuckered and we ain't even done anything.'

Dix kept both his hands on his holstered gun grips. He was as tired as his friend but every sinew of his body was like the honed edge of a straight razor. If Walker or anyone else tried their luck with their .45s Dix would respond with lethal accuracy.

They turned a corner to where a glowing lantern hung just above a facade which had the word 'Hotel' painted upon it. Dix began to relax the closer they got to the hotel.

'Is that it?' Dan asked. 'Is that the hotel you rented us a room at? Kinda fancy.'

'Yep, that's the one I booked us into, Dan.' Dix nodded. 'I reckoned it looked a whole lot fancier than all of the others.'

'Looks clean,' Dan admitted.

'I sure hope so,' Dix said. 'I paid fifty cents for that room. I'd hate to have overpaid.'

They rounded a water trough and stepped up on to the boardwalk. As the two men neared the hotel the sound of approaching horse's hoofs pounding the ground echoed off the wooden street walls.

The noise shattered the otherwise silent section of town.

Both the star packers stopped in their tracks and listened to the approaching rider. Dix slid his fingers around the triggers of his guns. As he listened he ventured to a porch upright.

He turned his head and whispered to his partner.

'I can hear only one horse, Dan.'

Dan walked to the edge of the boardwalk and rested his knuckles on to his grip.

'Are you sure?' he asked.

'I'm dead sure,' Dix drawled. 'I can tell you that it's a long-legged horse and it's trotting this way.'

Dan rubbed his neck. 'How the hell do you figure it's a long-legged horse, Dixie? How can you be so damn sure?'

Dix moved away from his friend, raised his left hand and pointed out into the amber lantern light.

Dan looked flustered.

'Answer me, Dixie. How can you be so damn sure that it's a long-legged horse?'

Dix sighed and jabbed the air with his finger. 'Mainly 'cause I'm looking straight at the damn thing, Dan.'

10

The unearthly sound of the beating hoofs grew louder as both men stared at the tall animal trotting slowly through the cocktail of evening mist and amber lantern light. Its rider sat motionless as he steered the elegant animal down the centre of the street with unerring confidence. Dan and Dix drew their guns and aimed them at the approaching horseman. Dust rose up from the ground as the rider guided the high-shouldered stallion toward the lantern-lit hotel. Suddenly Dix lowered his guns as he stared in disbelief at the familiar figure astride the tall animal.

There was no mistaking the long mane of hair which bounced on the wide shoulders of the rider. The fringed buckskin jacket revealed the two deadly guns which rested in the specially designed holsters. There was no mistaking the elegant horseman to the eagle-eyed Dix.

'It's Hickok,' Dix gasped in astonishment.

Dan took a step forward.

'What in hell is Wild Bill doing in these parts?'

'He's heading right at us.' Dix dropped his .45s into their holsters and shook his head.

'I heard tell that he was in Deadwood,' Dan said as he holstered his gun. 'I wonder what he's doing here?'

'He'll tell us soon enough.'

Hickok pulled back on his reins and slowed his powerful horse as it closed in on the hotel. He stopped the stallion close to the water trough and looked down at the two men with stars pinned to their chests.

'Well, if it ain't James Butler Hickok,' Dix grinned.

'Well, I declare, if that don't take the biscuit,' Hickok said as he dismounted close to the water trough. He dropped his reins and looked at both his old friends. 'Two old men wearing stars. It looks like they'll hire any old fools in this damn town.'

'You might be right, James Butler,' Dix grinned.

Dan smiled broadly. 'What in tarnation are you doing in this territory, Wild Bill?'

Hickok allowed his mount to drink as he stretched his bones and looked at the hotel.

'I'll tell you what I'm doing in this territory. I'm looking for the varmint that hired a gunslinger to kill me, Dan,' he said as he pulled a long thin cigar from his buckskin jacket and bit off its tip. 'His trail led me right here. I figured the *hombre* who paid him his blood money must be living here.'

'What happened to the gunslinger, James Butler?' Dix asked as he ventured closer to the long-haired man.

Hickok struck a match, lit his cigar and then tossed the match aside.

'I killed him,' Hickok said as smoke

drifted from his mouth. 'It was the least I could do considering he was going to shoot me.'

Dix nodded. 'You say his tracks led you all the way here?'

'Yep, my friend.' Hickok inhaled more smoke and looked around the barren street. 'All the way to a damn town with all of its saloons closed for business. Where the hell am I?'

'This is Dead Man Draw, Wild Bill,' Dan replied.

'What kinda name is that for a town?' Hickok rested his knee-high black boot on the boardwalk and sucked on his cigar thoughtfully. 'Sounds like some drunk christened this place after shooting a corpse.'

'It does kinda sound like that,' Dan agreed.

'So you're here to find the man who hired the gunslinger?' Dix asked thoughtfully. 'This is a mighty big town.'

Hickok straightened up and looked at Dix.

'How many people in this mighty big town have got big wallets, Dixie?' he asked his old friend. 'It took a lot of money to hire Flint Conrad. The man I'm looking for has got himself real deep pockets.'

'Flint Conrad?' Dix repeated the name. 'He was fast with his gun and mighty expensive.'

'He wasn't that fast, Dixie.' Hickok inhaled on his cigar again and savoured its flavour.

Dix glanced at Dan and then back at Hickok.

'There's only three men in town that we know of who have more money than sense,' he noted.

'You're right, Dixie,' Dan agreed.

Hickok moved between his two old friends. 'Who would these three men be?'

'The men that hired us to be star packers, that's who,' Dan replied.

Hickok tapped the ash from his cigar. 'Have they got names?'

Dan rubbed his jaw. 'I don't want

you to go killing folks just 'cause they're rich enough to hire a gunslinger, Wild Bill.'

Dix smiled. 'James Butler wouldn't go off half-cocked, Dan. He wouldn't kill anyone until he knew for sure that they were the guilty party.'

'Is that right, Bill?' Dan asked the tall, pale-skinned man with the mane of long brown hair. 'You wouldn't go and kill them men just 'cause they're rich enough to be the bastard that hired Flint Conrad, would you?'

'Nope, not until I was sure that I'd found the man that had hired Flint Conrad.' Hickok smiled. 'Then I'd kill him real happily.'

'The three rich dudes in town are Boris Day, Lucas Smart and Stu Rogers,' Dix informed his old friend. 'I sure hope you don't kill them before me and Dan get paid.'

Hickok gave a wry nod of his head.

'I can't promise nothing, boys,' he said as he turned and picked up his reins and moved to his horse. 'The guilty party has to die otherwise he'll not rest until I'm dead.'

'Are you sure?' Dix asked.

'I'm dead sure.' Hickok stepped into his stirrup and mounted the stallion. He gathered up his reins and steadied the mount. 'Flint Conrad told me that just before he died. He said that the man that hired him would not rest until I was dead. I believe him.'

Dan rubbed his chin.

'I reckon I would as well,' he agreed. 'I've never known any dying men that lied just before they went to meet their Maker.'

Hickok placed the cigar between his teeth. 'Flint Conrad told me that his paymaster would just hire another gunslinger if he didn't fulfil his obligation. I have to stop this at its source. There ain't no other way.'

Dix looked up at the elegant horseman.

'Where are you going now?' Dix asked. 'Most places in town are closed.'

Hickok smiled and touched the brim

of his hat. 'The kind of places I frequent are usually open for business this time of night, Dixie. I'll see you in the morning.'

Both the lawmen watched as the high-shouldered stallion carried its master into the main thoroughfare. They turned away from the edge of the boardwalk and started toward the hotel door.

Dan sighed heavily as he pondered. 'Where do you figure he's going, Dixie?'

Dix led his partner into the hotel.

'It sure ain't a prayer meeting, Dan,' he wryly smiled.

11

Tom Dix watched the sun rise from his hotel-room window with more than a hint of trepidation tracing through his veins. No matter how hard he had tried to sleep during the night it had been a futile exercise. He had risen an hour before the last star faded from the night sky and watched as the golden orb had bathed Dead Man Draw in blinding light.

The light streamed in through the hotel window and warmed the room instantly. Dix wandered from the window to his bed and stared down at his hand-tooled gun belt with its twin holsters. The pair of matched Colts rested there as though waiting for their master's hands to animate them.

Even though he knew why Day and his partners had hired them, Dix knew that there was more to this job than simply pinning on stars and collecting money.

There was danger looming. Dix could sense it as easily as he felt the warmth of the sunlight which brought the small room to life. He rubbed his tired eyes and glanced at his sleeping friend. Then he suddenly thought about Hickok and wondered if fate had brought their old pal to this remote settlement. There was no reason for the famed gunfighter, gambler and some-time lawman to be anywhere near Dead Man Draw and yet he was here.

Over the years their paths had crossed many times and for a supersti-tious man like Dix, there had to be a reason. What strange unseen power had guided Hickok to this town at this exact moment?

Whatever had brought James Butler Hickok here, Dix hoped it was a good omen. The first time they had all bumped into one another Dix and Dan had been young. The passage of time had not been kind to them whilst

Hickok still looked almost the same.

A smile crossed Dix's unshaven face as he thought about the flamboyant Hickok. There were very few men who could scare a man to death by simply walking straight at them with his guns drawn, but James Butler could.

Dix turned and lifted his gun belt from the rickety chair beside his cot. He strapped it around his lean hips and secured its silver buckle.

He patted his flat belly and glanced across the room at the other bed and his slumbering friend. Time had not been kind to either of them but Dan seemed to be feeling his age more than Dix lately.

They had set out in a vain bid to outride civilization and leave it behind them in search of the true Wild West before it disappeared altogether.

Dead Man Draw might be the very place they had been seeking and yet Dix was starting to regret their trek. The trouble with lawless places was that they tended to be merciless.

The only law was gun law. A man had to be fast with his guns if he was to survive and someone like Dix himself was only as good as his last showdown.

He flexed his fingers and tried to get the stiffness out of his knuckles as he glanced back at Dan. How long would he survive if something happened to him? Dix wondered.

Although Dan had spent years working as a lawman, he knew nothing of the true magnitude of situations like this. Dan was a good soul who should have retired to a rocking chair by now, Dix thought.

Dix wondered why the old lawman had chosen to ride with him instead of taking that far easier option. He checked both his .45s before moving around his own bed to where his pal still slept.

He leaned down and shook his pal's shoulder.

'You awake?'

Dan opened his eyes and stared up at the once famed gunfighter. He smiled and rubbed his eyes.

'What time is it, Dixie?' Dan asked as he threw the sheet off him and placed both his feet on the bare floorboards.

Dix turned back to the window and paced toward it.

'Early,' he muttered.

Dan yawned and then grabbed his pants. 'Has anything happened, Dixie?'

Resting his back against the window Dix replaced the spent shells of his six-shooter with fresh bullets from his belt.

'Nope, not yet anyways,' he replied.

Dan buttoned his pants and then put on his boots. He was watching his pal closely. It had been a few years since he had seen Dix looking quite so edgy.

'How come you're up so early, Dixie?'

Dix slid his gun into its holster and then pulled its twin free. He began to check that one as well.

'I reckoned it might be best if we got an early start.'

Dan nodded as he rose to his feet and picked up his vest from the chair and put it on.

'You're probably right.' Dan lifted his own gun belt and strapped it around his girth. 'What do you figure our first move should be?'

Dix holstered his gun and then leaned down and started to tie the leather laces around his thighs.

'Breakfast.' He said what he knew Dan wanted to hear.

Dan grinned. 'Now that's what I call a plan, Dixie. A real good plan.'

Dix picked up his deputy star off the dresser and pinned it to his chest. He watched his partner do the same with his sheriff's badge.

Both the lawmen left their room and made their way down the corridor to the top of the staircase. As always Dan trailed Dix. The hotel was quiet as they made their way down the carpeted steps to the lobby.

A sleeping man at the desk did not notice them walk out.

Dix paused and surveyed the street.

Dan looked at his pal. 'How come you're so nervous, Dixie?'

Dix smiled.

'Habit I guess. They reckon you never see or hear the bullet that kills you but when I was a gunfighter I learned real early it don't pay to take any risks.'

Dan adjusted his hat.

'Let's go find that café,' he said. 'That big female might be lonely. She had a hankering for you, Dixie.'

'She didn't.' Dix blushed.

'I might be wrong but I reckon she likes old-timers,' Dan laughed.

The two lawmen wandered slowly along the boardwalks which fronted so many of the buildings in Main Street. Even though the sun was rising in the blue cloudless sky only a handful of people were up and about.

Dix was still watching out for trouble, though. No matter how hard he tried he could not shake off a lifetime of being a gunfighter. Every corner held the possibility of a back-shooter waiting for his unsuspecting target.

Dan walked a half-step behind the watchful gunfighter and kept staring at his friend. He knew that Dix never truly relaxed. It was as though he was unable to permit himself that grace. He always walked with his hands resting upon the grips of his matched .45s.

The walk took them the better part of ten minutes. They glanced at the large stone-block building as they passed opposite it. There was no sign of the three businessmen at this ungodly hour.

A few steps more and they reached the café.

Dan shielded his eyes from the bright sunlight which was reflecting off the café window and peered in through one of its glass panes.

'It looks like it's open, Dixie,' he informed his friend before sniffing the aromatic air. 'Smells like she got the griddle all fired up as well.'

Dixie nodded as his eyes darted around them. He saw a few men getting their stores ready for business. A red and white pole caught his attention. He rubbed his whiskered face.

'Remind me to head on over to the barber shop and have a shave, Dan,' he said as he turned and followed Dan into the café. He closed the door behind them.

Dan sat down at the same table they had used the night before and dropped his hat on to a spare chair.

'Not until you've filled that belly of yours,' he said. 'I've never seen a grown man who eats as little as you.'

'I'm not real hungry, Dan,' Dix said as he took his hat off and looked out through the window.

Dan pointed at the star on his vest.

'Sit down and get ready to eat,' he told Dix. 'I'm the sheriff and you're the deputy. I outrank you. You're eating and that's an order.'

Dix toyed with his Stetson and sat down. He was about to speak when the well-proportioned female appeared from the rear of the café. When she saw Dix her eyes lit up. She began to navigate between the tables and chairs toward them.

She smiled and Dix leaned back on his chair. When she reached the table she leaned over Dix. He tried to divert his eyes from her low-cut cleavage and the generous amount of flesh nestled there.

'Nice to see you again, Deputy.'

'Howdy, ma'am.' Dix blushed.

'You must like my cooking,' she said, leaning over to give him an even better view of her assets.

'I sure do,' Dix beamed.

'My pal was thinking about having himself a shave, ma'am,' Dan told her before asking, 'Do you reckon my pal Dixie needs a shave?'

Her soft hands stroked his whiskers. Her long eyelashes fluttered.

'I surely like hair on a man's face.' She purred like a kitten.

'You do?' Dix looked surprised.

'I sure do,' she said as she gently tugged on his whiskers. 'I don't like men with faces that look like a baby's bottom.'

Dan cleared his throat and vainly tried to get her full attention. 'I reckon I'll have steak and eggs for breakfast, ma'am.'

She leaned even closer to Dix and enquired, 'What do you want, Dixie?'

'I'll have the same, ma'am,' Dix stammered.

'You can call me Polly.' She pinched his cheek. 'You want coffee with your meal, Dixie?'

Dix slowly nodded.

'Thanks, Polly.'

She stroked his face seductively.

'My pleasure.'

Both men watched silently as she returned to the rear of the café. It was as though she was walking on air. This time she not only swung her hips, she was also singing.

Dix looked at his friend. 'What you grinning at?'

'I told you.' Dan winked. 'She's sweet on you.'

Dix exhaled.

'What kinda sheriff are you anyway? You're supposed to protect your deputy,' he snorted.

'You best eat all your grub, Dixie,' Dan teased. 'I reckon that you might need all the strength you can muster.'

12

At the far end of Dead Man Draw three other men awoke early just like the lawmen. Unlike the two star packers they were not hungry for food. Their appetite was for something far more deadly. Their hunger was for greed and blood-spilling, for they craved the small fortune that Day, Rogers and Smart had regularly collected from each of the businesses in town. They had another craving gnawing at their innards as well. This one was more permanent.

They wanted the very lives of the trio of businessmen who worked out of the large stone building and they were prepared to take them.

Nothing could stop them.

Greed chewed at their craws. Walker had suddenly realized that in this lawless town all a man needed to become rich was guns and the willingness to use them.

Killing had always been easy for Walker. Now it was also profitable. All he had to do was keep killing and soon he would own the entire town itself.

He had never shied away from shooting anything or anyone but now he had more than enough reasons to vent his dubious skills and lay claim to everything the businessmen had. They were the only thing that stood in his way.

They would die as easily as the others, he told himself.

Their deaths would prove far more profitable, though.

Walker moved to the doorway of his shack and stared out across the dusty road to the mass of buildings surrounding the tall grey edifice. He rubbed his jaw eagerly and looked back at his two cohorts.

'Are you ready, boys?' Walker growled, before checking his arsenal of weaponry.

Green and Lee ambled out into the morning sun and donned their hats. They stared at Walker and knew that he would lead them to a fortune.

'We're ready, Jody,' Lee said as he grabbed the reins of his horse and drew it toward him.

Green pulled his long leathers free of the pole he had secured them to the night before. He looked through blood-shot eyes at Walker and forced a smile.

'You got yourself a plan, Jody?' he asked.

Walker gave a firm nod and rested his hands on the guns on his hips.

'I sure have got me a plan, Frank.' He laughed and went to his horse. He grabbed hold of its mane and merci-lessly pulled the animal toward him. He mounted and looked at the sun-bleached rooftops of the town. 'I plan to kill Day and his fat friends and take control of this town. Look at it, boys. It's ready for plucking.'

Cautiously Lee and Green mounted and watched as Walker glared with insane eyes at the town.

'What about the money in your saddle-bags, Jody?' Lee asked the deadly killer. 'Are you gonna leave it in your shack?'

Walker looked at Lee.

'Why the hell not, Duke? Before the sun goes down tonight we'll have us a hundred times that amount of money. Like I told you, we'll be the richest critters in the whole damn territory.'

The faces of Lee and Green suddenly sobered up as Walker's words drilled into them. Lee moved his mount close to the horse of Walker.

'Do you figure we can do it, Jody?' he asked.

'It'll be like taking candy from a baby, Duke.' Walker smiled. 'So easy it'll be embarrassing. I never seen a town so damn defenceless as this one is. I killed the sheriff and his deputy and nobody even raised an eyebrow. I killed Pete Mason in the saloon and the place was packed. Nobody did a thing.'

'And now you intend killing Day and

his pals?' Lee asked.

Walker looked crazed as he nodded.

'Damn right. There's nobody in Dead Man Draw with the guts to stand up against me. When Boris Day and his two partners are dead we'll be in charge.' Walker laughed. 'We'll have the contents of their safe and we'll do all the collecting of dues.'

Green leaned over his saddle horn. 'I like this plan. I really like it a lot, Jody.'

Walker nodded.

'C'mon, boys. Let's go and get rich.'

They laughed and then spurred.

13

There was a small, affluent section of Dead Man Draw where a handful of its wealthier citizens resided. It was a leafy street with white picket fences which would not have looked out of place in far more civilized towns back east. The houses were spacious and unlike any of the structures found in the rest of town. To live here you had to be rich and the three men who ruled Dead Man Draw from the grey stone-block building in Main Street were rich enough.

Their homes were close to one another which suited not only Day but Smart and Rogers as well. As the sun's rays filtered through the canopy of trees along the avenue Stu Rogers marched toward Boris Day's home at pace.

He pushed the gate open and hurried up the paved path to the large front door. With terror blurring his wits

Rogers beat upon the door.

'Open up, Boris,' Rogers repeated over and over again.

Boris Day looked up from his dining room table and patted his lips with a napkin. He rose to his feet and made his way toward the front door. The large man grabbed his tailored coat and put it on before he turned the door handle and pulled it open.

'What's gotten into you, Stu?' Day asked as he looked at the flustered figure before him.

'I have to tell you something, Boris,' Rogers said. 'Something really important.'

'Couldn't it wait?' Day asked. 'You'll see me at the office in about an hour. I don't understand.'

'An hour might be too late.' Rogers glanced fearfully over his shoulder as if he expected someone to strike at him from the bushes. 'I gotta tell you something right now.'

'Then spill it, Stu,' Day sighed. 'I ain't finished my breakfast yet.'

'I was in town earlier and someone told me that Walker critter killed someone else after we all went home last night, Boris,' Rogers stammered. 'I rushed here to tell you.'

Day narrowed his eyes.

'Who did Walker kill?'

Rogers was shaking. 'He killed Pete Mason at The Broken Spur. Walker put two bullets into him and collected the monthly dues. He might have killed even more but we ain't heard about it yet.'

Day lifted his hat from the wall rack and looked down at it in his hands.

'Damn. I was thinking that maybe Walker killed Sheriff Davis and his deputy by accident.' He sighed. 'Now it looks as if the idiot has his mind set on killing everyone that pays us dues.'

Rogers mopped his brow.

'That's what I thought, Boris.'

'Walker has sure been blatant about his killing,' Day said. 'He don't give a damn who knows it's him pulling the trigger.'

'I've been thinking,' Rogers said nervously. 'What if Walker ain't content with just collecting the money from the saloons, Boris? What if he has bigger ambitions? What if he comes after us?'

Boris Day suddenly looked as troubled as his partner. He glared at Rogers.

'I hadn't thought about that, Stu,' he confessed. 'That does kinda put this in a different league.'

'That loco Walker might decide to finish us off and help himself to what's in our safe,' Rogers added. 'Our lives ain't worth a plug nickel if he gets to aiming them guns of his a little higher. He might figure on killing us and taking over our operation.'

Day rubbed his jowls and fumbled for a cigar inside his coat. He located a fat Havana, bit off its tip and placed it in his mouth. He struck a match and sucked its flame into the cigar.

'You could just be right, Stu. Walker might get the notion that if he gets rid of us then he'll be free and clear to do anything he chooses,' Day reasoned through a cloud of tobacco smoke.

Rogers swallowed but there was no spittle.

'I'm scared and I ain't ashamed to admit it.'

'We'd better go and warn Lucas about this.' Day adjusted his hat and left his house. He closed its door and started down to the white picket fence with Rogers at his side. 'If we're right, Walker might get the idea to pick us off one by one.'

As they reached the gate Rogers grabbed Day's sleeve as he remembered something else. Day stopped and looked at his partner.

'What?' Day asked.

Rogers was like a scared jackrabbit. He looked all around the street for any sign that the man he feared would soon turn his weapons upon them.

'I just remembered something, Boris. Lucas ain't ever home at this hour,' he said as he pulled his golden hunter from his pocket and flicked open its cover.

'If he ain't here then where the hell is he?'

'By my reckoning he'll be halfway to the club by now to have himself breakfast, Boris,' Rogers said. 'He always has breakfast there before going to the offices.'

'I didn't know that.' Day thoughtfully puffed on his cigar.

'He might walk straight into Walker.' Rogers trembled. 'We gotta warn him.'

'There's no time to hitch up the buggy, Stu. We'll have to walk there as fast as we can,' Day said firmly.

'I'm nervous being out here in the open with Walker still roaming around, Boris,' Rogers admitted. 'We need the guards who are protecting our safe at the office. We need them here to protect us.'

'Quit fretting, Stu,' Day said. 'At least the guards are protecting our safe. Besides, we just hired a new sheriff and deputy.'

Rogers shook his head.

'Them two old guys can't protect us

and you know it,' Rogers ranted. 'We only hired them to do our money-collecting.'

They were walking faster than either of them had done for several years. Day was sweating like a pig.

'Dan Shaw used to be a lawman,' Day argued. 'I got me a feeling they're more than just money collectors.'

'I sure hope you're right,' Rogers stammered.

The two alarmed men hastened their pace down through the leafy street toward the heart of Dead Man Draw. Although Day would never admit it, he too was scared.

14

The brothel was less obvious than most of its competition in Main Street. It did not have any fancy signs outside or highly decorative facades advertising its wares. The faded brown boards which covered the front of the whorehouse were as bland as the rest of those dotted along Main Street. The only clue to what went on behind the closed door was a solitary lantern hung from its porch with a piece of red silk draped around its glass.

Only a determined man who knew what he was looking for would have even noticed the lantern during the hours of darkness.

Hickok had found it easily.

The tall figure had satisfied his cravings and now was standing by the hotel window allowing the sun to warm his pale skin. Hickok rested his hands on the frame of the window and watched the activity in the street as all men of his profession watched. Ever since he had first gained notoriety Hickok had never been able to relax like other men. There was always someone who wanted revenge or a young buck that wanted to make his name by being the one who outdrew the living legend.

For years Hickok had sought solace in the arms of any female who agreed his price, a bottle of whiskey or the relative safety of a marathon poker game.

Yet it was a vain quest.

No matter how hard he tried to ignore the danger of simply being the man known as Wild Bill Hickok, he knew that he was doomed to eventually fail.

He had created a flamboyant image for himself that set him apart from most men who roamed the west. It was a calculated attempt to frighten the majority of potential killers away but he knew there was always one who might be blind to his bravado.

The fictional stories of his exploits in countless dime novels had only added to his troubles. They had made him famous but they had also made him a target in the eyes of those who wanted to make him little more than a notch on their gun grip.

Hickok realized that the man who killed the famed Wild Bill would be doing so in an attempt to steal his thunder. He sighed and stared at the men and women who moved along Main Street and wondered what it would be like to just be one of them. To be invisible and not noticed by anyone apart from someone who knew his life depended on being observant.

But he had invested too much effort into his image to abandon it now, he thought.

For better or worse he was Wild Bill.

There was no expression in his face as his hooded eyes darted from one person to the next as they went about their daily rituals far below his high vantage point.

Some said Hickok had the perfect poker face. Only a handful of people had ever been able to tell what mood he was in. Neither happiness nor gloom etched his strangely smooth features.

He ran his fingers through his mane of long hair and was about to turn back to the female in the bed when he caught sight of two dazzling stars pinned to the chests of the pair of men leaving the small café.

Hickok lowered his head and watched Dix and Dan.

He narrowed his hooded eyes and stroked his moustache with his trigger finger.

'My, those tin stars sure make good targets,' he muttered.

'What did you say, Wild Bill?' the soft voice asked from behind his shoulders.

Hickok looked at her.

'I didn't say anything for you to worry your little head about, Sally,' he smiled.

She sat up in the dishevelled bed and looked indignant at the slim pale figure.

'My name happens to be Gloria,' the female argued.

He gave a slightly mocking bow.

'I apologize for my mistake, Gloria.' Hickok picked his shirt off a chair and started to put it on. He moved around the room like a caged tiger. 'I was thinking of another town and another sweet dove.'

She watched his every movement. 'Where are you going, Wild Bill? I thought we were going to spend all day having fun.'

Hickok started to button up the shirt.

'I've two old friends I have to talk with, Gloria,' he said. 'I'll be back though, unless I get tangled up in something tricky.'

She wrestled with the sheets on the bed and stared at him as his thin hands lifted up his fancy shooting rig. He looped the unique belt around his hips and buckled it on his hip. The two pearl-handled gun grips poked out from their crossed holsters.

'Are your friend's better company than me, Wild Bill?' she asked the famous figure. 'Are they?'

He looked at her as he tied the leather laces around his thighs. He raised an eyebrow.

'Nope but I'm kinda hungry.'

'We could get food sent up here,' Gloria suggested.

'I'm kinda thirsty as well.'

Gloria lifted the empty whiskey bottle and then shrugged as she lay back on the pillows.

'Reckon you're just the same as all the other johns that come here visiting me.' She sighed sorrowfully. 'You have your fun and then you high-tail it.'

Hickok pulled on his hefty buckskin and finally placed his flat-brimmed hat on to his head. Her naked form was a temptation but it was not enough to prevent him leaving.

He touched his hat brim and moved toward the door.

'You're wrong. I'm nothing like all

the other men that visit you, Gloria,' he said before tossing a golden fifty-dollar coin on to the bed.

Her small hands grabbed the coin.

'What makes you so different?'

He turned the key and opened the door.

'I'm Wild Bill Hickok,' he drawled. 'The one and only.'

15

Main Street was now sweltering. Shimmering heat rose from the numerous water troughs as the rays of the rising sun found their contents. As unseen clocks continued to tick the morning away, the street became filled with people. From one end to the other they appeared. Men on horses rode in and dismounted as well-covered females moved from store to store carrying wicker baskets. Exactly like every other town in the territory Dead Man Draw had awoken from its slumbers to start a new day and forget the previous one.

It was as though no blood had been spilled.

For whatever reason, this town was exactly the same as all of its contemporaries. It chose to forget the things that frightened it.

Only those with courage remembered.

The two star packers had only just reached the well-disguised whorehouse when Dix paused. He was chewing on a toothpick as he led his partner toward the side of the building. They both glanced up the alley.

'What you so darned interested in, Dixie?' Dan asked.

Dix stepped into the shadowy alley and looked to what was at the far end of the wooden structure. He spat the toothpick from his mouth and rested his hands on his matched pair of six-shooters.

'Look.' Dix pointed.

Dan shuffled closer. 'I'm looking.'

'Don't you recognize it?' Dix asked.

Dan rubbed his chin and then patted his pal on the back heartily. 'It's just a horse, Dixie. If you hadn't noticed, the street is full of the things.'

Dix looked at his friend.

'The street ain't full of thoroughbred stallions like that one, Dan,' he noted.

'That's James Butler's nag.'

Dan took another look. A smile filled his features as he began to nod in agreement.

'So it is.'

Just as they were about to continue on their way, the side door of the building opened and a familiar figure stepped out into the shadows.

There was no mistaking Hickok. They had never known anyone else who dared to sport knee-high black boots.

'Howdy, boys,' he drawled and he closed the door behind him. 'I thought I heard two old hens clucking. I should have realized it was you.'

'Wild Bill,' Dan greeted. 'I ain't seen you up this early in a long while.'

Hickok stopped and looked at his old friends. He touched his hat brim and nodded.

'I wanted to have me a talk with you boys,' he said. 'I was just coming to see you two.'

'I don't believe in coincidence, James

Butler,' Dix said. 'You knew we were passing.'

Hickok nodded. 'You're right, Dixie. I saw those tin stars catching the sun and reckoned on rounding you up before some hothead used you for target practice.'

Dix moved to the side of the elegant figure and looked him up and down as was his habit.

Hickok glared with his hooded eyes at his old friend.

'Have you seen enough, Dixie?'

Dix grinned. 'Yep. You're still as fancy as you ever was, James Butler.'

Hickok touched his hat brim. 'Thank you kindly, Dixie.'

'Last night you told me and Dan that someone had paid a hired gun to shoot you. Is that what you was coming to see me and Dixie for, Bill?' Dan asked as the flamboyant man walked out into the sunshine and inhaled the morning air deeply.

Hickok did not answer. He turned and glanced up at the high windows instead. His hooded eyes stared at the one he had just left the female in.

'I asked you if you was hankering to talk about the varmint that hired that killer, Wild Bill,' Dan repeated. 'Well, are you?'

Hickok raised an eyebrow.

'I did reckon on you boys knowing who might have enough money to hire someone as expensive as Flint Conrad.'

'We're new in town but we got an idea,' Dan said.

Dix rubbed his whiskers and looked at the room window which Hickok seemed interested in.

'What was she like?'

'She had vinegar, Dixie,' Hickok noted.

Dan tilted his head and looked at the tall figure.

'I figure you're looking for a poker game,' Dan asked. 'Am I right?'

'Nope, you're wrong, Dan.' Hickok turned and started to walk across the street. His two old friends followed.

Dan and Dix looked at one another

before returning their attention to Hickok as he strode across the dusty street toward a saloon.

'Then you're going to drink a saloon dry,' Dan laughed.

Hickok paused as his boot heel rested on the boardwalk. He lowered his head. His hooded glare looked at both the lawmen through the strands of his long hair.

'Somebody in this town hired Flint to kill me, boys,' he growled. 'I wanna find out who that galoot is.'

Dix pushed his hat off his brow.

'Then what, James Butler?' he asked.

Hickok pulled out a thin black cigar from his buckskin pocket and placed it between his teeth.

He ran a match down a porch upright.

'Then I'm gonna kill him.'

Both men watched as Hickok touched the end of his cigar and blew out a line of smoke. He tossed the match at the sand and then stepped up on to the boardwalk.

He continued walking.

'We can't let you just murder someone in cold blood, Bill,' Dan uttered.

'Don't try to stop me, boys,' Hickok said. 'It wouldn't pay.'

16

Totally unaware of the dangers which were smouldering in and around Dead Man Draw, Lucas Smart made his way down the narrow alley next to the grey block building toward the small private club he and his partners had built for the more affluent of the town's menfolk. Unlike either Rogers or Day he had no servants in his large home and took all his meals in the quiet surroundings of the club. As he crossed the alley toward the entrance he checked his pocket watch.

He had made good time. Smart resolved he had time to have two cups of coffee with his breakfast. He moved briskly down the street toward the one place where rich men could gather without being troubled by lesser mortals.

As Smart reached the stone steps he

paused and pulled out his silver cigar case and removed its lid. The businessman had only just extracted one of his specially imported smokes when three large shadows moved across the tall wall of the club. He made the mistake of ignoring the ominous black shapes.

Smart placed the cigar between his teeth, returned the case to his coat pocket and patted himself down in search of a match when he noticed the shadows before him had halted.

He curiously looked at the red brick wall and yet was not alarmed by the dark images upon it.

Eventually Smart found a match and scratched it down the wall and enclosed its flame in the palms of his hands. As he drew in the smoke he looked at the three shadows more closely and noticed that they were the shadows of three riders.

Each of them had stopped behind him.

He exhaled a cloud of smoke and then became aware that the shadows remained stationary for a lot longer than seemed normal.

Smart turned and stared into the rising sun.

It was hard to see anything with the blinding rays of the sun directly behind the three horsemen. He puffed and raised a hand to shield his eyes.

For a moment his curiosity got the better of him.

Like a sheep to the slaughter Smart naively advanced toward the horsemen. The three riders sat astride their mounts twenty yards from the club.

Smart had only taken two steps when his shielded eyes focused on the lead rider. He recognized Walker. A wave of terror washed over him as he paused in his tracks at the unexpected sight which faced him.

He went to speak but it was too late.

The sound of guns being cocked filled the quiet area.

Suddenly Lucas Smart recalled seeing Walker as he blatantly moved from killing to killing the day before.

Every sinew in his body realized that he was facing the very same man who had killed mercilessly just to get his hands on the saloon money.

Smart rubbed the sweat from his jaw.

Then Jody Walker drove his blood-stained spurs into the flanks of his mount and rode to within ten feet of the startled businessman.

The morning sun dazzled Smart as it reflected off the two six-shooters in the horseman's hands.

'Walker,' Smart gasped.

A sickening laugh filled the air.

'That's right, Smart,' Walker chuckled.

'I ain't done you no harm,' Smart stammered. 'You can have all the money you can collect. I'll not stop you.'

Walker enjoyed making his prey squirm.

'I know you won't,' he hissed.

Smart looked up at the horseman. He knew that it was pointless trying to talk sense to a creature like Walker. He was intent on doing what he liked and nothing could deter him.

'Say howdy to Satan for me, Smart,' Walker said as he aimed his .45s.

Smart hastily backed away. He tried to run but his legs would not obey him. He raised his hands.

'Don't shoot, Walker,' he begged. 'Don't shoot.'

Walker turned to his cohorts and joked.

'It sure looks like Smart is damn scared, boys.' He laughed hideously at his defenceless target. 'Anybody would think I'm gonna kill him.'

Green and Lee laughed out loud at the sight of the terrified businessman.

'Kill him, Jody,' Lee urged. 'Blow his stinking head off his shoulders.'

'Put him out of his misery,' Green laughed.

Walker returned his full attention to the traumatized businessman. He kept waving his .45s at Smart.

'He sure don't look so important now.' Walker hissed like a sidewinder. 'I reckon that all his money is weighing him down, boys.'

Smart desperately glanced at the alley and then over his shoulder at the entrance of the club. He was unarmed but knew that meant nothing to men like Walker. His breed killed for the sheer pleasure of it.

'Please. I ain't got no gun, Walker,' Smart said as he backed away from the horseman who kept urging his mount toward the fearful man.

Walker grinned.

'That don't mean nothing to me, Smart.'

Smart knew that if he remained in the open Walker would undoubtedly kill him. If he were to give himself even a slim chance of survival he had to run. He had no option.

The well-dressed figure turned. Smart ran as fast as his shaking legs would carry him toward the entrance of the club. In all his days he had never moved so quickly. There was a real good reason for his speed. He was fuelled by fear. Just as Smart reached the first of the stone steps Walker squeezed on his triggers.

A pair of venomous bullets erupted from the barrels of his .45s and homed in on their target.

The alley resounded with the deafening sound of the gunshots. With smoke billowing from the barrels of his guns, Walker steadied his horse and watched Smart arch as the hot lead tore through his back.

He clawed at the air when the impact stopped his flight.

The bullet holes in his fancy suit soon darkened as blood spread across its expensive fabric. Smart fell on to his knees as life evaporated from his wounds. He turned to face the three laughing horsemen.

The dying Smart went to speak but only blood came from his mouth. The cigar fell from his lips and rolled to the sand at his feet. The look of utter shock was carved into the face of the horrifically injured Smart as he rested on the bloody stone steps.

Walker's cohorts moved their mounts closer.

'Look at the varmint twitch, Jody,' Lee laughed.

'He won't be twitching for much longer.' Walker cocked his six-shooters again and aimed them at the dying man.

He fired both his guns again.

The noise of the shots was amplified within the confines of the alley. It seemed to encircle the horsemen.

What life was left in the bloody figure of Smart buckled and then fell forward on to the sand as Walker's shots ripped into him. Gore covered the usually pristine stone steps. Its crimson traces ran down the steps like a waterfall.

Walker steadied his mount. He then heard an enraged voice coming from inside the club. The merciless killer cocked his guns and defiantly waited.

He did not have to wait long.

Plodding bootsteps filled the killer's ears.

'What's going on?' a voice bellowed from inside the club as a burly man came bursting out with a twin-barrelled shotgun clutched in his hands. The large man and Walker looked at one another. They both knew that one of them had to die. Before the huge figure had time to cock its mighty hammers Walker fired again.

The shots cut through the gunsmoke like rods of fork lightning and hit the big man dead centre.

The burly figure dropped his large weapon and then tumbled like a felled tree down the steps and on to the top of Smart's body. Lifeless eyes stared heavenward as the shotgun slid down after its dead owner.

Walker backed his horse away from the pool of blood which trailed from the club steps to the sand. He gave a grunt of satisfaction and his dark eyes stared gleefully at his handiwork.

'One down and only two to go,' Walker muttered.

'I ain't never seen such shooting,

Jody,' Green yelped as he steadied his horse.

'You killed them dudes real sweet, Jody.' Lee nodded in agreement. 'I reckon you must be the best shot in the whole damn territory.'

Walker holstered his still-smoking guns.

'This is just the beginning, boys,' Walker promised. 'I ain't even built up a head of steam yet.'

Powerfully, Walker turned his mount. He drove his spurs deep into the flesh of his horse and rode between Green and Lee.

'C'mon, boys,' he yelled out at them. 'We've got a lot more killing to do.'

Both Green and Lee slapped their long leathers across the tails of their mounts and followed Walker. For the first time since Walker had told them of his ambitious intentions they believed that he was capable of achieving his goal.

Within a few seconds of the deadly gunfire all that remained in the alley at the side of the large stone-block edifice was a cloud of hoof dust and gunsmoke.

That and two lifeless bodies soaking in a scarlet pool.

17

The deafening sound of the brief but deadly slaughter echoed all around the town just as Dix and Dan followed Hickok and were about to enter a welcoming saloon. Hickok had only just placed one of his hands upon the top of the swing doors when the noise of the execution greeted them. He turned and looked at the two star-packing men beside him and then ventured toward the edge of the boardwalk.

Dix walked to the side of the thoughtful Hickok. He had seen the tall man like this before.

'What you thinking about, James Butler?' Dix asked his slender friend.

'Just pondering on who fired them shots, Dixie,' he answered. 'Whoever it was they sure hit their target.'

Dix rested his hands on his grips. 'How can you tell that?'

Hickok glanced at Dix. 'I just know, old friend. How many shots did you hear?'

Dan strode to his friends. 'Three shots, Wild Bill. We heard three shots.'

'There were six shots from two guns,' Hickok corrected.

Dan Shaw looked at the tall motionless figure. He was about to argue when he realized that both his pals knew more about guns than he.

'You can tell that?' he sheepishly asked.

Wild Bill gave a slow nod. 'Yep.'

Dix turned to Dan. 'Go round up our horses, Dan. I got me a feeling that we're gonna need them.'

The man with the sheriff's star pinned to his vest gave a shrug and rubbed his sweating neck. He did not say another word. His two pals were veteran gunfighters and they knew more about this kind of thing than he had ever learned. If Dix said they needed their horses, that was good enough for him.

Dix watched as his friend started to hurry in the direction of the livery stable. He then edged level with the brooding Hickok.

'He's gone,' Dix said. 'I reckon it'll take him at least thirty minutes to saddle our horses and then collect your fine stallion from behind the whorehouse.'

Hickok turned his head.

'I figure thirty minutes is plenty of time for you and me to go find out who got themselves shot and who did the shooting, Dixie,' Hickok said before resting a hand on his friend's shoulder. 'We don't want Dan getting in the line of fire, do we?'

Dixie nodded. 'You can read me like a picture book, James Butler.'

'I know you got a soft spot for that old lawman,' Hickok noted. 'And you don't want him getting himself shot up no more than I do.'

'I owe him,' Dix sighed.

Hickok straightened up.

'And Tom Dix always pays his debts.'

The two gunfighters stepped down from the boardwalk and began the long walk to where they knew the shots had come from.

Every eye watched the two tall men as they walked down the middle of Main Street as though they were heading an army troop. But there was no troop of soldiers following them; they were alone. The sun was blazing down upon the pair of very different men.

There was no mistaking what they intended as they strode determinedly toward their unknown goal. All that the onlookers knew for sure was that this pair were on their side and that was all that counted.

18

Boris Day and Stu Rogers had just crossed the small bridge which spanned the meandering creek and entered the darker part of Dead Man Draw when the chilling sound of Walker's unanswered shots slowed their pace and quickened their heart rates. No sooner had they crossed the wooden bridge and set foot on the opposite side of the creek when Rogers stopped and anxiously bit his fingernails. The younger of the pair gripped the edge of the bridge and tried to stop shaking.

Day looked at his nervous associate.

'What you stopping for, Stu?' Day asked as he mopped the sweat from his rotund features and stared at his partner. 'We're nearly there.'

Rogers glanced in terror at Day.

'That's why I stopped, Boris,' he stammered.

Day removed his coat and draped it over his arm. 'I never reckoned on you being a yellow-livered coward, Stu.'

Rogers moved swiftly to his larger partner and grabbed his arms. He shook Day hard.

'I ain't no damn coward,' he yelled at his partner, 'but I ain't hankering to commit suicide either.'

Day looked down at Rogers's frantic expression.

'What's gotten into you, Stu?' he remarked. 'You're talking like a madman.'

'I'm no madman, Boris,' Rogers insisted.

Day peeled his partner's hands off him and brushed himself down angrily.

'Then what's wrong with you? I thought you wanted to try and get to the club so that we could warn Lucas of the possible danger, Stu.'

Rogers looked at the ground and exhaled loudly.

'That was before I heard those shots, Boris,' he said shakily. 'We both know what those shots mean. It means that Lucas bumped into Walker.'

Day straightened up and mopped more sweat from his face.

'Those shots could have come from anywhere, Stu,' he guessed. 'You're jumping to conclusions. For all we know Lucas is sitting over a plate of ham and eggs right now.'

'I tell you they came from Walker's guns, Boris,' Rogers yelled loudly. 'Who else would be fanning his hammer at this time of the morning?'

Boris Day looked into the town. 'Are you saying you reckon Walker has just killed Lucas?'

'That's exactly what I'm saying.'

'Let's make our way down to the office and find out,' Day suggested. 'We can't hide here. I reckon Walker will mosey on over here to kill us before he tries to snuff out Lucas's candle.'

'Walker's already snuffed out Lucas's candle, Boris,' Rogers insisted.

Day became hesitant. 'You might be wrong, Stu. There's gotta be a dozen other folks that could be shooting their guns off. The town is full of drunks. Any one of them critters could have been firing aimlessly. It don't mean Lucas is dead. It just don't.'

Rogers chewed on his fingernails. 'It might, though. What if I'm right?'

Day took another few steps and stared at the massive livery stable at the edge of the town. He then saw the sun reflecting off the tin star on Dan's vest.

'Look, Stu.' He pointed excitedly. 'I see just the man we need to talk to.'

Rogers nervously moved toward Day and squinted. 'What the hell are you pointing at?'

Boris Day tossed his coat over his sweat-soaked shoulder and led his partner to where they could see the massive livery stable at the very end of Main Street. His index finger stabbed the air.

'Look, Stu,' Day urged.

Rogers screwed up his eyes. 'I don't see anyone.'

'I've just seen one of our new

lawmen,' Day insisted. 'He went into the livery stable. If we hurry we can catch up with him and ask if he's seen Lucas.'

'Which one of them did you see?' Rogers questioned.

'I reckon it was the sheriff,' he said. 'Anyway, it was one of them. I saw his tin star. Are you coming, Stu? He'll know if anything has happened to Lucas or not.'

Reluctantly Rogers agreed even though every sinew in his being was screaming out for him to run for his life.

'OK. Let's go see if the sheriff knows anything.' He nodded.

Both men started to run as best they could across the rough sandy ground toward the tall weathered structure. It was the first time either of them had moved faster than walking pace in years.

The interior of the livery was cooler than the rest of Dead Man Draw and a welcome relief to anyone who had endured the morning sun. Unaware that both Dix and Hickok had sent him to collect the horses because they feared for his safety in a gunfight, Dan made his way to the well-built blacksmith and touched his hat brim.

'Howdy, friend,' he said as his eyes searched for the two horses Dix had left there the previous evening. 'I'm looking for two nags. My partner left them here last night.'

The blacksmith was sitting beside the glowing coals of the massive forge as if he were immune to the heat it generated. The big man looked at the tin star and then raised an arm and pointed to the far corner.

'They're both over in the far corner, Sheriff,' he said as his gleaming muscles flexed. 'What's eating at you? I never seen a star packer look as troubled as you before.'

'There's a murderous killer in town,' Dan said. 'I'd have thought you already knew that.'

The blacksmith levelled his stare at

the lawman and then gave a nod of his head.

'You're going up against Jody Walker, ain't you?'

Dan smiled. 'I reckon.'

'You and your pal look mighty old but I got me a feeling that you have to be pretty good at your job to live as long as you two have,' the blacksmith said. 'You'll get him and the scum that ride with him.'

'Much obliged for your confidence,' Dan said. 'Can you help me get these horses saddled up? I'm in a real bad hurry.'

'If'n I was you I'd bide my time looking for Walker,' the blacksmith said.

'There's trouble in town, friend,' Dan informed him as he led his own horse from its stall. 'Me and my pal are trying to stop Walker from killing any more folks.'

The blacksmith seemed unimpressed. 'A lot of folks try to quiet things down in Dead Man Draw. A lot of men end up in Boot Hill.'

Dan threw his blanket on to the back of his horse and patted it down.

'A lot of folks ain't got Wild Bill Hickok in their corner,' he added. 'I'm sure Hickok will be mighty thankful if you help me.'

The blacksmith looked up at the sheriff and stood. He moved quickly for a big man across the livery to the stall next to the one Dan had just led his mount from. His big hands untied Dix's horse from its stall and walked him out and started to ready the rested animal.

Dan looked at the blacksmith, who placed a blanket on the horse's back.

'Thanks, friend.'

'Is Wild Bill in town?' the blacksmith asked as his muscular arms lifted a saddle on to the back of the horse. 'Is he really here in Dead Man Draw?'

Dan nodded. 'He sure is, friend.'

'Golly, I always wanted to meet that dude.'

Dan was about to speak again when the sound of hurried footsteps caught his attention. He drew his gun as one of the stable's tall doors rocked as the two businessmen raced into the structure.

'Your kinda nervous, ain't you?' the blacksmith commented as Dan slid his six-shooter back into its holster.

'Yep. I sure am,' Dan admitted and continued to saddle his horse as the two sweat-soaked figures moved through the livery toward them.

'What was all the shooting we heard, Sheriff?' Day asked.

Dan secured his cinch strap and then lowered his saddle fender. He looked at both men. They were bedraggled by their own sweat and looked nothing like they had done only the previous day.

'I sure wish I could answer you,' Dan said as he watched the blacksmith tighten his partner's cinch. 'We intend to find out, though.'

Rogers moved closer to the veteran lawman.

'Have you seen Smart?' he asked.

Dan shook his head. 'Nope, we ain't

seen nobody. I came to get the horses so we could try and round up whoever it is doing the shooting.'

'You're sure you ain't seen Smart?' Rogers pressed.

'I'm sure.' Dan grabbed the saddle horn and stepped into his stirrup. He eased himself up on to his saddle and gathered up his reins as the blacksmith handed him the long leathers for Dix's mount. 'We heard the shooting and Dix told me to get our nags.'

'Find out everything you can, Sheriff,' Day insisted. 'My partner thinks that Walker might have killed Smart. He has a vivid imagination.'

Dan looked down at Rogers. 'You might be right about Smart. I'll find out, though.'

'Then it was Walker who did the shooting earlier,' Rogers said in a shaking voice.

'It sure looks that way.'

Rogers clenched his pale fists and cursed at the dirt beneath his feet. 'I damn well told you, Boris. Why the hell didn't you listen to me? Until Walker's dead our lives ain't worth a dime.'

'Calm down, Stu,' Day gulped.

Dan touched his hat brim and spurred toward the large open doors. He led his partner's mount out of the livery and into the bright morning sunlight. The sound of pounding hoofs filled the weathered structure as Dan rode away.

The blacksmith leaned over the far shorter men.

'I'll bet you didn't know that Wild Bill Hickok is in town. He's helping the sheriff and his partner,' he said, before heading back to his glowing forge. 'Walker don't stand a chance against Hickok.'

'Hickok?' Rogers repeated the name and looked at Day in bewilderment. 'What in tarnation do you figure he's doing in this town, Boris?'

A look of horror filled the sweating face of Day as he clutched his jacket. The rotund figure walked to a large water bucket and used a tin cup to scoop himself a drink and then rested the cup down.

Rogers looked at his partner. Day suddenly looked as scared as he had only moments earlier.

'Do you know why Hickok's in Dead Man Draw, Boris?' he asked Day.

Day gritted his teeth and nodded.

'He's looking for someone,' Day replied.

'Who?' Rogers asked.

'He's looking for the man that hired Flint Conrad to kill him, Stu.' Day sighed heavily and mopped his face for the umpteenth time.

'Who would hire a back-shooter like Conrad?' Rogers wondered.

'Me,' Day answered.

'But why?'

'I've got my reasons to want Wild Bill dead, Stu.' Day swallowed the bitter taste in his mouth. 'It looks like Hickok's a whole lot better with his guns than I figured. Maybe some of them stories I read about Wild Bill are closer to the truth than I thought.'

'Wild Bill must be real good with his guns if he killed Flint Conrad,' Rogers stated. He glanced at the sweating Day. It was like looking at a man walking to his own hanging. The difference was that Day feared his hangman would come in search of him to seek revenge.

19

The sight which greeted the two gunfighters might have turned the guts of most men but neither Dix nor his tall, elegant companion was surprised. They had both witnessed far worse in their lives. There was not a hint of any emotion in the poker-faced Hickok as his hooded eyes looked down at the pair of bloody bodies. His mane of long hair beat like the wings of a powerful eagle on his buckskin-covered shoulders as a breeze cut up through the alley. The famed gunfighter slowly raised his head and stared at Dix without uttering a word. Then Hickok turned on his heels and surveyed the alley.

'What you thinking about, James Butler?' Dix asked as he gripped one of his six-shooters in his hand.

The flamboyant figure stepped over the bodies and stood before Dix. He pulled out a cigar and placed it into the corner of his mouth thoughtfully. His long slim fingers slid a match from his shirt top and scratched its tip with his thumbnail.

Dix eased himself closer to his famed friend. He was still amazed how calm Hickok always appeared to be. Like so many men who had endured the long, brutal war no situation ever seemed to disturb the tall, slender man.

Hickok tossed the match into the pool of blood at his feet and blew out a line of smoke.

'There were three of them but only one did the shooting, Dixie,' Hickok elaborated.

Dix tilted his head. 'Three?'

Hickok nodded and turned. His pearl-handled gun grips poked out from their holsters to either side of his belt buckle. The tall man gave a nod of his ageless head.

'That's what the tracks say, Dixie.'

'I'd only figured on there being one,' Dix admitted.

Hickok savoured the flavour of his long thin cigar. 'We only got one to trouble ourselves over. The other two *hombres* are just hanging on his shirt tails.'

Not one part of their surroundings escaped scrutiny as Dix looked all around them. Yet no matter how hard he tried he could not see any sign of the men they sought.

'Where are they?' Dix asked angrily.

Hickok calmly pulled the cigar from his mouth. He looked up at the rear of the massive stone-block building and then pointed his cigar at it.

'In there,' he replied. 'Leastways that's where they intend being before too long, Dixie.'

Dix did not understand. 'What do you mean? They're either in there or they ain't.'

Wild Bill raised an eyebrow.

'I reckon by the look of that massive eyesore that building is full of money, Dixie,' Hickok assumed. 'The *hombre* that killed these folks wants that money

163

real bad. He intends getting it and if he ain't stopped he will.'

Dix sighed. He knew his emotionless friend was right.

Hickok aimed his cigar down the alley. The rising light of the merciless sun cascaded on to the backs of a half-dozen buildings. Hickok was pointing to the very end of the alley but then looked at the grey building next to them again. The bars on its lower windows drew his attention.

'They rode down the alley, Dixie. I reckon they're a tad thirsty but after they get themselves quenched they intend busting into that big ugly building and stealing themselves every penny that's inside it,' Hickok said thoughtfully.

'So you reckon they're in a saloon?' Dix pressed.

'That's where I'd be,' Hickok admitted. He returned the cigar to his mouth and then gave a flick of his head for Dix to follow. Dix watched as Hickok started to walk to where the hoof tracks led. As his knee-high black boots ate up the ground Hickok drew one of his guns, cocked its hammer and looked over his shoulder at Dix.

'If you want to stay healthy stay close, Dixie,' Hickok drawled.

Dix followed Hickok as the tall figure trailed the hoof tracks left by Walker and his cohorts. James Butler Hickok had once been an army scout and it was said that he could track better than most men could spit.

The two men had barely reached the furthest of the sun-drenched buildings when Hickok suddenly stopped and slowly turned.

'What's wrong?' Dix asked his tall friend.

Hickok kept his .45 at his side as his long fingers pulled the cigar from his lips and dropped it to the sand. He did not answer his old friend as his hooded eyes narrowed against the blinding rays of the sun. The tracks led on for another two hundred or more feet but Hickok ignored them. He was staring up a narrow gap between two of the buildings instead.

He glanced at Dix.

'They've gone all the way around, Dixie,' Hickok informed his pal. 'They're already up on Main Street.'

'Are you sure?' Dix asked.

'Damn sure,' Hickok replied.

A sudden realization dawned on Dix. He grabbed the arm of his friend and turned the tall man around to face him. It was an act of bravery that only Dix could achieve without getting himself filled with lead.

Hickok looked at his pal's worried face.

'What's eating you?' he asked.

'Dan!' Dix exclaimed.

'What about him?' Hickok asked.

Dix pointed his drawn gun.

'I just thought. Dan will be riding back down Main Street with our damn horses at any moment,' Dix said anxiously. 'If Walker and his pals are there, Dan will ride blindly straight into their bullets. Walker and his buddies will mow him down. He'll be a sitting duck.'

Hickok frowned.

'You're right,' he said earnestly. 'Another thing, that damn tin star Dan's sporting will make a real good target for someone as useful with his guns as Walker is, Dixie.'

'We gotta stop Dan before he rides into Walker and his cronies,' Dix said.

Suddenly, without warning, the sickening sound of a deafening volley of shots echoed all around the alley. Both gunfighters knew where they had originated.

Main Street.

'Those shots came from Main Street,' Dix said as he swung around and looked in the direction of the thoroughfare. More shots rang out. 'The bastards are shooting at Dan.'

The tall figure in the fringed buckskin jacket gritted his teeth and began to run to where they had heard the shots.

'C'mon, Dixie,' Hickok shouted, as

he raced toward the narrow gap between the pair of wooden structures. 'There ain't no time to lose.'

More shots followed. Wild Bill Hickok reached the street before his friend and paused against the wooden wall of a storefront. A line of smoke hung in the sunlight on the still air directly ahead of him. The experienced gunfighter sniffed the air. It was gunsmoke, he thought. Nothing smelled as bad as gunsmoke.

Dix reached his side and pressed himself up against the opposite wall of the narrow, litter-strewn alley they had feverishly negotiated.

'You took your time,' Hickok joked as he removed his flat-brimmed Stetson and dropped it on to the sand. 'You ought to grow longer legs, Dixie.'

'Any idea where they are?' Dix asked.

Wild Bill Hickok pointed his drawn gun to his left.

'They're up there somewhere,' he said. 'Leastways that's where all the bullets are coming from.'

'Has Dan returned fire?' Dix asked.

Hickok shrugged. 'Nope.'

Desperately Dix leaned out and peered around the wooden wall in the opposite direction. His heart missed a beat when his narrowed eyes spied Dan on the ground just beyond the body of one of their horses.

'Dan's down,' Dix croaked, as he focused on the bloody scene. 'He ain't moving. He ain't moving a muscle.'

Hickok narrowed his eyes to where his friend was looking. The carcass of the saddle horse was closer than the motionless sheriff. A pool of blood was spread around both horse and rider. It glistened like precious jewels in the sun-drenched street.

He reached across the narrow gap and pulled Dix back.

Dix turned and looked at the taller man.

'He ain't moving,' Dix repeated.

'I know, Dixie.'

Before either of them could say another word a volley of shots whizzed past them again. They watched red tapers cut through the sunlight. They listened as each bullet connected with the prostrate mass of horse flesh.

Hickok could see the bullets bury themselves into the stricken horse.

'Luckily for Dan that dead horse is soaking up their bullets, Dixie,' Hickok mumbled as his mind tried to calculate what the best course of action should be.

He carefully looked around the corner to his left. The street was filled with choking smoke. He could see the three horsemen but there were a dozen porch uprights blocking any clear targets.

'They're all shooting now,' he said before looking up at the porch above the storefront. For a moment Hickok just stared at it before a notion came to him. He turned to his shocked friend. He held Dix's shoulder and shook him violently. It was his crude way of bringing his friend back into full activity.

Dix pulled free. 'What you do that for?'

'Are you any good at climbing, Dixie?' Hickok asked as he aimed his gun at the porch overhang. 'Can you hitch yourself up there?'

'I reckon I can,' Dix answered the strange question.

'Fine. I knew you still had vinegar.' Hickok stretched his long lean frame up and then took hold of the shingle tiles. He then scrambled up the wooden wall of the store and came to a rest upon the porch roof. He lay on his belly and offered Dix a helping hand. 'C'mon. We ain't got all day.'

Hickok hauled Dix up on to the sloping porch.

The street was thick with gunsmoke as the two men moved across the porch roof. Hickok stepped off the sloping overhang on to the balcony of The Broken Spur saloon swiftly trailed by Dix.

The putrid smoke from the continuous gunfire shielded their movements from the eyes of Walker and his cohorts. Both gunfighters advanced on the three horsemen.

Unlike the porch shingle roof the balcony was level and fronted by a wooden rail which spanned its length. As the gunfighters got to the very end of the balcony Hickok raised his hand and stopped.

Dix held his six-shooter in one hand and rested his other on the rail. Both he and Hickok looked down from their high vantage point. Through the swirling smoke they could see the trio of horsemen taking pot-shots at their helpless target.

Wild Bill forced Dix backwards on the balcony until they were both halted by the saloon's second-storey wall. Dix glanced at his pal.

'What you doing?' he asked.

'How good are you at flying, Dixie?' Hickok raised an eyebrow.

'I'll give anything a try, James Butler.' Dix nodded.

They bolted across the balcony to the

rail, stepped up on to it and then leapt like mountain lions. They dropped through the gunsmoke with their guns in their hands.

Hickok's boot heels hit Frank Green clean off his mount. A mere heartbeat later Dix landed on top of the unsuspecting Duke Lee. Both of Walker's cronies hit the sand hard.

Dix smashed his gun across the neck of the already unconscious Lee as Hickok rolled off the dazed Green. For the first time since the shooting had started Jody Walker was not laughing. He swung his mount around and looked at the familiar figure of Hickok rising up through the dust cloud.

Green pawed at the sand and found his gun. Hickok fired one sweet shot and Green was knocked off his knees and thrown into the side of a trough. Blood spread from the fatal wound in his chest.

Walker steadied his horse and trained his guns on the long-haired figure in the buckskin jacket.

'Wild Bill Hickok?' he gasped in disbelief.

'That's what they call me.' Hickok staggered to his feet and went to cock his gun.

Walker raised his smoking guns.

'Say your prayers.'

Walker squeezed both triggers and then realized that his hot weaponry needed reloading. He desperately threw one .45 at the tall figure. It caught Hickok in the temple and stunned him.

With his other gun clutched in his hand Walker swung his mount around and spurred. Dix rose to his feet and steadied Hickok as blood trailed down his face.

They watched as Walker's mount jumped over the bullet-riddled horse and the still-motionless Dan.

Hickok shook the spent casings from his gun and reloaded as Dix aimed his gun. He fired and then watched as Walker continued to ride away.

'He's out of range of my damn .45,' Dix cursed before he looked at Hickok.

Blood trailed from Wild Bill's hairline as he snapped his gun chamber shut. 'Are you OK?'

'I'm fine, Dixie,' Hickok snarled. 'I'm a tad angry, though.'

Dix started to run toward Dan and then heard one of the horses snorting behind him. As he ran he looked back and saw Hickok grab the reins of Lee's horse and throw himself up on to its saddle.

Just as he reached Dan, Dix watched as Hickok thundered past him in pursuit of Walker. He fell down beside his pal as the long-haired rider vanished from view into the cloud of hoof dust.

Boris Day and Stu Rogers were standing beside one of the tall livery-stable doors staring down into the heart of the long street when suddenly they heard the sound of hoofs approaching them. Through the shimmering haze they saw the desperate flight of Jody Walker as he vainly tried to reload his gun as he steered his lathered-up mount toward the stables.

'That's Walker!' Day exclaimed.

'You're right.' Rogers backed away but knew there was nowhere to go. He stopped. 'We're dead men.'

Day looked all around him. He dropped his jacket and ran back into the large interior of the stable.

The blacksmith looked up from his forge at the face of the fat old man.

'What you looking for, Day?' he smiled.

Day glared at the seated blacksmith. 'You've got guns in here. Where are they? Give me a damn gun.'

'Find them,' the blacksmith taunted. 'I'll not stop you.'

The sound of the horse being reined in filled the livery stable. Day turned and looked at his partner bathed in sunlight. He watched as Rogers raised his hands.

Walker stopped his mount a few feet away from Rogers. Then he saw Walker finish loading his gun and fire directly down at his helpless target.

Rogers was knocked off his feet.

Day stood like a petrified statue as his unblinking eyes saw Rogers float backwards leaving a rainbow of bloody droplets in his wake.

Then Walker leapt from his horse and ran into the livery stable.

'Get me a fresh horse, blacksmith,' he yelled before he saw Day standing in a puddle of his own sweat in the centre of the straw-strewn floor. He skidded to a halt and smiled at the terrified man. 'If it ain't Boris Day. Just the man I wanted to kill.'

Day raised his hands in a vain bid to stop Walker's bullets.

'You can have every damn penny in the safe, Walker,' Day stammered before tossing a large key across the floor. 'That'll open our safe. Take it all. Just spare me.'

Walker stooped and plucked up the key. A cruel smile etched his face.

'I hate to do this after your generous gift but . . . '

The dim interior of the livery stable lit up as Walker fired a shot into the ample girth of the businessman. Day tilted forward and fell on to his knees.

The killer's smile vanished as the sound of an approaching horse's hoofs echoed around the livery. Walker gritted his teeth, slid the key into his pants and cocked his gun again.

Hickok dragged the reins back as he reached the dying Rogers stretched out before him. Suddenly a shot flashed from the dark belly of the livery and narrowly missed him. Faster than he had ever moved, Hickok dropped from the unfamiliar animal and crouched behind it. His hooded eyes narrowed as he squinted into the stable.

He saw Walker standing before the kneeling Day.

Hickok grabbed the bridle of the horse and forced it into the stable. He slapped the animal's tail and then ran behind it into the large structure.

Walker stepped to the side and then saw Hickok roll across the dirt floor. He fired and then saw a bright flash erupt from the barrel of Hickok's six-shooter.

Jody Walker did not hear the deafening shot which echoed around the livery stable. He was already dead. Hickok got to his feet and strode across the floor to the livery and briefly glanced at Walker before turning his attention upon the kneeling Day.

It was obvious to Hickok that Boris Day was a dead man although he still breathed. He watched as Day lifted his head and looked at him.

'I'm the one you're looking for, Wild Bill,' Day said as blood trailed from the corner of his mouth. 'I hired Flint Conrad.'

'Why?'

Day's eyes rolled in their sockets. 'That you'll never know.'

Hickok watched as Day fell on to his face. His secret died with him.

He looked at the blacksmith and sighed.

'Damned bastard died before I could kill him,' he complained.

The blacksmith nodded. 'Ain't it always the way?'

20

Tom Dix sat on the steps of the doctor's small office and looked up at the unmistakable figure of Hickok as the tall man walked down Main Street toward him. Hickok paused as he reached Dix.

'How's Dan?' Hickok asked.

'He's still alive,' Dix replied.

Relieved, Hickok nodded. 'Good.'

The door of the doctor's office swung open and the weathered old medical man made his way down toward the two watchful men.

Dix rose to his feet and turned to face the doctor.

'Is Dan OK, Doc?'

Doc Hardy gave a small nod of his head. 'He will be when he wakes up. I sewed his wounds real tight.'

Dix rubbed his neck. 'What happened to him?'

'He got winged by three bullets.' Doc Hardy sighed. 'One skimmed his temple. Knocked him clean out. Lucky really 'cause he was limp when he fell from his horse. A man of his age usually breaks his neck after a fall like that. Yep, he's sure a lucky critter.'

Hickok tossed a golden half-eagle into the hands of the doctor.

'Thank you kindly, Doc,' Hickok said.

'Thank you.' Doc Hardy returned to his office.

Dix nodded to Hickok.

'Thanks for paying for that,' Dix nodded. 'Me and Dan are a little shy on money. That's why we took the jobs as lawmen.'

Hickok looked around him. 'Where do you reckon my long-legged horse went, Dixie?'

Dix smiled. 'He's somewhere around here, old friend.'

'He'll show up soon enough I guess.' Hickok pulled the large safe key from his pocket and studied it. 'Bad pennies always show up eventually.'

Dix looked at the key between Hickok's fingers. 'What's that you got there, James Butler?'

Hickok raised his eyebrows. 'Just something that fell out of Walker's pocket.' He shrugged. 'Reckon I'll see you later after I see what it opens.'

Dix watched as Wild Bill Hickok started to walk toward the tall grey-stone building. He then caught up with his pal and tagged along beside him.

'I guess I'll walk with you for a spell.'

'Where are you headed, Dixie?' Hickok asked his companion.

'I'm just going to get me some vittles,' Dix replied with a glint in his eyes. 'There's a real nice woman in the café who likes me.'

Hickok patted the key against his moustache. 'Do I know her, Dixie?'

'I sure hope not,' Dix laughed. 'I sure hope not.'

We do hope that you have enjoyed reading this large print book.

Did you know that all of our titles are available for purchase?

We publish a wide range of high quality large print books including:
Romances, Mysteries, Classics
General Fiction
Non Fiction and Westerns

Special interest titles available in large print are:
The Little Oxford Dictionary
Music Book, Song Book
Hymn Book, Service Book

Also available from us courtesy of Oxford University Press:
Young Readers' Dictionary
(large print edition)
Young Readers' Thesaurus
(large print edition)

For further information or a free brochure, please contact us at:
Ulverscroft Large Print Books Ltd.,
The Green, Bradgate Road, Anstey,
Leicester, LE7 7FU, England.
Tel: (00 44) 0116 236 4325
Fax: (00 44) 0116 234 0205

QUICK ON THE DRAW

Steve Hayes

Luke Chance has one claim to fame: he's real quick on the draw. Trying to outrun a reputation he doesn't want, he ends up in Rattlesnake Springs — where he meets the beautiful Teddy Austin. Teddy hires him to break horses on her father's ranch, but pretty soon Luke is locking horns with the Shadow Hills foreman, Thad McClory. As if that wasn't enough, the Austins are also having trouble with their neighbors. Though he doesn't want to get involved, it seems Luke can't help but do so . . .